Intensive Care

Debby Fowler

A Felicity Paradise crime novel

D0238553

ISBN 978 185022 214 9

Published by Truran, Croft Prince, Mount Hawke,
Truro, Cornwall TR4 8EE
www.truranbooks.co.uk

Truran is an imprint of Truran Books Ltd

This novel is a work of fiction. Names and characters
are the product of the author's imagination and any
resemblance to actual persons, living or dead, is entirely
coincidental.

Printed and bound in Cornwall by R. Booth Ltd,
Antron Hill, Mabe, Penryn, TR10 9HH

Acknowledgements
As always I would particularly like to thank Jo Pearce
for deciphering my scribbles. I would also like to thank
Sally Gilbert and Charlie Fowler, faithful couriers, the late
Tony Stevens and his brother, Nigel for the cover, Ivan and
Heather Corbett for their encouragement and patience,
and of course, my husband and children.

www.felicityparadise.co.uk

For Tony
A good man, sadly missed

1

September 2003, St Ives, Cornwall

'Mum, I need money for the taxi.'

'What?' said Felicity, staring stupidly at her tall, blonde daughter standing in the doorway, supporting a truly enormous suitcase.

'Taxi money, Mum, I've no cash left. It's outrageous, he wants thirty pounds just to bring me from Truro station, it's daylight robbery.' Dangerous blue eyes flashed with indignation.

'You should have stayed on the train until St Erth, except there wouldn't have been any taxis there at this time of night …' Felicity's voice trailed away. What on earth was Mel doing in St Ives, without warning and with a suitcase large enough to contain her whole life?

'Mum, please!'

'Sorry, sorry,' she said, 'let me get my purse.'

Between them they lugged Mel's case through the front door of Jericho Cottage, hampered by

Orlando, Felicity's ancient cat, who was clearly outraged and bristling with fury. The case took up the whole of the hall and they had to clamber over it to reach Felicity's tiny kitchen. Once there, they turned to face one another.

'Well, it's lovely to see you Mel, darling, if a little unexpected.' Felicity tentatively held out her arms. Mel had never been demonstrative with her mother, hugs had been reserved for her father, so it was to her great surprise that Felicity found herself not only hugging her daughter but being hugged back. They disentangled and Felicity looked thoughtfully at her. Something was clearly very wrong. 'So darling, are you here for long or are you just passing through?' she asked with a touch of irony, glancing past her daughter to the monstrous suitcase.

'I don't know,' Mel replied, avoiding eye contact.

Another first, Mel always knew everything. She was the most certain person Felicity had ever known. She felt a slight stirring of panic and then mercifully the maternal instinct to nourish kicked in. 'What can I get you, darling, something to eat, coffee, tea or a glass of wine?'

'A large brandy, please.'

'Are you sure?' asked Felicity, involuntarily. Mel had always been rather critical of her parents' drinking habits, particularly those of her father,

2

Charlie. She believed that drink and the law didn't mix. Charlie had taken great pleasure in citing famous drinking lawyers through the centuries to fuel Mel's indignation.

'Yes, I'm quite sure, thank you,' replied Mel, giving her mother a steely look. Felicity found brandy glasses and the remains of a bottle of Hennessey.

'Let's go through to the sitting room,' she said, 'the fire should still have some life in it.'

The cosy sitting room was still warm. Felicity threw a log on the fire, Mel poured the drinks and they sat on the sofa beside one another. Orlando clambered up between them. So huge was he that once he had satisfactorily arranged his bulk, the two women were perched on the outer edges of the sofa. Neither argued, Orlando's tyranny was too well established.

'So what's going on, Mel?' her mother asked.

'I've been sacked, Mum.'

Felicity stared at her daughter. 'I simply don't believe you.'

Mel took a sip of her drink, swirled the brandy around in her glass, staring down at it. 'Well, not sacked exactly, but that crap idiot Jeremy Powell has been offered the tenancy instead of me.'

'But he can't have been taken on instead of you, that's absolutely ludicrous!' This was not simply maternal pride speaking, it was plain common sense.

On leaving university with a first class law degree, Mel had been offered articles by a crack law firm in Lincoln's Inn. She had been articled to Michael Ferguson, a young barrister who, without doubt, was destined to be a QC before his fortieth birthday. Everyone had assumed Mel's star was linked to Michael's, her future assured. Certainly, her father had thought so.

'You may consider it ludicrous but I can assure you, Mum, Michael has taken on Jeremy instead of me. We were both interviewed but I assumed it was just for form's sake. Obviously, I was very wrong because Jeremy's got the job.' The desolation in Mel's voice made her mother's heart twist.

'But why Mel, why? It makes absolutely no sense.'

Mel sighed and looked up at her mother almost shyly. 'Michael says it's because Jeremy fits in better with the firm. He's a 'yes man' of course, but that's presumably what they want, someone who will make no waves, upset no one, do as he's told,' she paused, 'I think Basil may have had a lot to do with it.'

'Basil?' Felicity queried.

'Our clerk, he hates me. He never gives me any decent briefs, he always favours Jeremy.'

As the widow of a barrister, legal politics were not lost on Felicity. 'It doesn't do to fall out with the clerk, Mel, you should know that. How on earth did that happen?'

'I don't know, we've just never got on.'

'You can be rather forceful,' Felicity suggested, 'and somewhat opinionated on occasions. Maybe you just rubbed him up the wrong way and didn't show enough respect. Clerks have a difficult job – they're neither one thing nor the other, but they are so terribly powerful within chambers.'

'Please don't start,' Mel almost shouted, 'you're supposed to be on my side. Why can you never stick up for me, Mum? It's always been the same, hasn't it? Darling Jamie, the boy wonder, can do no wrong, but Mel only has to put one foot out of line to be criticised. Why can't you support me for once, rather than assume it's all my fault?'

The words hung in the air between them. Felicity stared into the glowing embers of the fire, desperately trying to think of the right way to reply. It was true, Jamie, Mel's brother, had always needed extra encouragement throughout his childhood. Having to cope with an outgoing, popular, academically brilliant little sister who, without doubt, was his father's favourite meant Jamie had needed a lot of extra mothering. Too much, Felicity wondered? Clearly Mel thought so. She dragged her eyes away from the fire and met Mel's angry gaze.

'I have always been on your side, darling, and I always will. If it appears that I have sometimes favoured Jamie, I'm sorry. It's just that you were always so capable and until he mercifully met Trish,

5

his life was always such a struggle.'

'So when did you decide to like Trish?' Mel asked aggressively.

'Since your father died,' Felicity answered truthfully. 'I've done a lot of thinking about so many things, and his death changed my perspective on just about everything. I've come to really appreciate Trish. Jamie would be an absolute lost soul without such a supportive wife. She's stronger than him, he's cleverer than her – they have a pretty perfect partnership. They work well together, they play well together, they love their boys, I envy them their ...' Felicity struggled for the right word, '...their completeness.'

'You've changed your tune,' Mel said, grumpily.

'I have, but we're not here to talk about Jamie and Trish. I'm just trying to absorb what you've said. They haven't sacked you, just passed you over. Presumably you can just stay on another year or so and see what happens?'

'I've resigned, Mum.'

'You've what?'

'I've resigned. There is no way I'm going to stay on after this, it would be too humiliating.'

'But what is resignation going to do to your career?'

'I don't know and I don't care. I've just had enough. I've worked so hard, Mum, ever since I took my GCSE's. Four A Levels, no gap year, university,

6

articles, I've never stopped and where has it got me? Nowhere and yet I'd make a far better barrister than Jeremy, I know it.'

'I wonder what your father would have advised?' Felicity said, suddenly. For a moment, at the thought of Charlie Paradise, both his wife and his daughter were silent and united by his memory.

'He would have walked out too,' Mel said, 'no doubt about it.'

Felicity looked up and smiled. 'Mel, you're absolutely right.'

Normally when Mel came to stay with her parents they found the whole experience exhausting. During the day she was either on the telephone or e-mailing someone, she rose early, went to bed late – it was like a whirlwind through the house. Therefore it came as a great surprise to Felicity, the following morning, to find Mel was still asleep at nine o'clock, or apparently so. Certainly, there was no sound from the downstairs bedroom where last night they had finally dragged her enormous bag.

It was something of a role reversal, for it had been Felicity who had slept little during the night worrying about her daughter. This was the first family crisis she had faced alone. It was over a year now since her husband had died. She knew that in many respects she was starting to cope quite well with life alone but this was something else. If it had been Jamie in a crisis, she found herself thinking, I would have been able to deal with it so much better, I would have known instinctively what to do. This thought in itself brought on a wave of guilt. Until last night, it had never occurred to her that Mel, the gifted one, the golden girl, could possibly be jealous of her quiet, unassuming brother; Jamie was a self-confessed 'anorak', committed to his IT world, hopeless at sport, bullied at school, socially inept and underrated by his father. Mel, by contrast, had never needed her mother's protection, she had always been so capable, so grown up, far more grown up than Felicity herself would ever be. Had she misjudged the situation all these years? Was this apparently high-achieving, confident daughter masking a vulnerability that Felicity, until now, had never seen?

Having paced around her little cottage until she was almost giddy, she made herself the third cup of coffee of the morning, which on normal days was absolutely forbidden, went upstairs and out on to the balcony. At the now familiar sight of the harbour bathed in golden early autumn sunshine, Felicity let out a sigh of relief and sat down feeling the tranquillity of the scene wash over her. After a lifetime in Oxford, Felicity's friends saw her flight to St Ives as an attempt to run away from her husband's sudden death. They could not have been more wrong, Felicity thought. While at the time she had believed herself to be very content with her life in North Oxford, strangely, this funny little cottage tucked up behind the harbour, felt more of a home than any place she had ever lived in before. Why, she could not begin to analyse, but here at last she felt truly at peace. Maybe, she thought hopefully, some of that St Ives magic would wash off on her troubled daughter.

It was nearly ten by the time Mel arrived on the balcony. With hair all over the place and eyes puffy from her huge sleep, she still managed to look gorgeous. Felicity smiled at her with pride. She was a beautiful girl, having inherited the best of both of them – Charlie's height, her own colouring and somehow the mix and match of their features had worked perfectly. Why on earth hadn't Michael Ferguson wanted to keep her on, surely she had to be such an asset?

The idea, which had plagued her half the night, had to be voiced. 'You weren't having a fling with Michael, were you?'

'He's married, Mum.'

'I appreciate that, but he would hardly be the first married man to succumb to the charms of a beautiful work colleague. You do represent a serious temptation to any man, darling.' She smiled and was rewarded by a slight smile back.

'I haven't had time for men,' Mel replied, 'haven't had for ages, not since university really. I've been wedded to my job,' her face clouded, 'was wedded to my job.'

As she spoke, Mel studiously avoided eye contact. I've got a little too close to the truth for comfort, Felicity thought. 'Something doesn't stack up,' she said, patting the chair beside her. Mel sat down.

'There's no mystery, Mum. I upset people. I always have done but particularly since Dad died, I've been even more aggressive. I know it, I just can't help myself.'

'You must miss him?' Felicity said.

'Terribly,' Mel agreed, 'don't you?'

'Of course,' said Felicity, 'it's just in a weird sort of way I feel I might be coping with his death better than you, even though I was his wife.'

'Did you have marriage problems? Is that what you're saying?' Mel asked sharply.

Felicity shook her head. 'No. Sadly at the time of his death we were arguing over the Carver case, the case that killed him, but we were fine really.'

'You don't sound sure?' said Mel. She looked shrewdly at her mother for a moment. 'I've always wondered if you told us everything about Dad's murder. I had this very strong feeling that you and Josh were holding something back from me and Jamie.'

Felicity shook her head vehemently hoping that God was not about to send a thunderbolt to strike her down. It was a justified lie, particularly at the moment when Mel was so vulnerable. Maybe one day it would be right to tell her that the father she hero-worshipped had accepted bribes and lived a lie since before she was born, but Felicity could not imagine a time when such a disclosure would ever be appropriate.

Mother and daughter spent a domestic morning. Mel unpacked, or rather spread her clothes around the spare room. Like many highly intelligent people with organised minds, Mel's domestic skills were nil. Felicity prepared a casserole for supper and at lunchtime they wandered down to the Sloop Inn and enjoyed a crab sandwich and a glass of wine in the sunshine.

'I can see why St Ives grows on you,' Mel admitted, grudgingly, 'but compared with Oxford, it's something of a backwater. I can't see you being here forever, Mum.'

'I am here forever,' said Felicity, realising the truth of her words as she spoke them, 'and it isn't a backwater, it's a sort of microclimate. All of life is here, it's just in miniature. I love it.'

It was while they were sitting over coffee that Mel announced she was going for a walk after lunch. 'I'm going to walk to Zennor, on the coastal path' she said, 'and back, of course.'

'That's quite a hike,' said Felicity, 'it's a round

trip of at least twelve miles, Mel.'

'I know,' said Mel, 'I've just been talking to a guy behind the bar who says it's a great walk. It sounds just what I need.'

'Would you like me to come too?' Felicity asked faintly.

'Absolutely not, I'll be fine Mum. I just need to clear my head.'

'The evenings are drawing in,' said Felicity. 'I don't want you stumbling about on the cliff path in the dark.'

'I've got nearly five hours of daylight,' said Mel, 'don't fuss.'

Back in her cottage Felicity tried to settle down to some work. She had been commissioned to illustrate the book of a local author and she had been doing quite well, but today she just could not concentrate. After several abortive attempts she gave up. Leaving the front door unlocked in case Mel returned before her, she walked the few hundred yards to Cormorant Cottage and Annie Trethewey. Her former landlady and friend was predictably in the kitchen.

'What's wrong, my bird?' said Annie, without turning around.

'Nothing,' said Felicity, 'why should there be?'

'Because these days you only come to see me when there's something wrong.'

'Not true,' said Felicity, smiling. 'I come to see you every time I find I'm missing you, which actually is quite often for some reason, given what a beastly old baggage you can be on occasions.'

'Tea?' Annie asked, clearly unaffected by Felicity's description of her.

'Please,' said Felicity. Felicity watched affectionately as the tiny, birdlike figure of Annie flitted around her kitchen and deposited a teapot and a plate of chocolate brownies on the table. 'Take them away at once,' said Felicity, 'you know I can never resist your brownies.' Annie predictably ignored her and sat down opposite her. She poured the tea and then looked up at Felicity.

'So, are you going to tell me what's up?'

'I suppose so,' said Felicity, unfairly exasperated at Annie's perception. 'Mel's come home. She came home in the middle of last night.'

'Your daughter Mel?' Annie asked.

'Of course,' said Felicity, 'who else?'

'It's just that she's hasn't been down here at all, except when you first moved in and that was only for a day or two.'

'Judging by the size of her suitcase it's going to be a lot longer this time,' said Felicity. 'She's lost her job.'

'I thought she was a lawyer, a barrister, I think you said.'

'A baby barrister,' Felicity said. 'She's been

articled to a firm in London and the next stage, after you've been a pupil, is to be offered a tenant in chambers. Everyone, including Mel, expected her to move effortlessly to the next stage, but she's been passed over.'

'Why?' Annie asked, frowning.

'I'm not sure. I can't get to the bottom of it. The other pupil in line for the position is a rather colourless chap. She says she upsets people, which is why he got the job, not her.'

'She didn't strike me as a very happy person,' Annie said, 'what little I saw of her.'

'Really?' Felicity looked concerned.

Annie leaned over and patted her arm. 'I'm sorry, my girl, I don't want to upset you. She just seems something of a lost soul. Close to her dad, was she?'

'Very,' said Felicity.

'That explains it then – delayed grief – she needs to grieve for him properly. She has probably been denying the pain for months and been perfectly horrible to everybody around her to cover up her feelings, hiding them from herself as well as everyone else.'

'Annie,' said Felicity, 'are you sure you didn't train as a psychiatrist at some point during your chequered career?'

Annie smiled. 'Native cunning, my girl, that and a long life. You give that girl of yours plenty of home cooking and mother love – she'll be right as rain in a week or two.'

The sun was setting when Felicity finally left Annie's cottage and rather than go straight home, she wandered along the Wharf. It was such a beautiful evening, the sea ranging in colour from pale blue through to dark crimson as the sun sank. She leant on the railings and breathed in the salty air. Annie was right, as usual, she would do everything she could to give Mel the maternal affection she clearly felt she had lacked. She loved her daughter, it was just that she had always played second fiddle to the relationship between Mel and her father. Suddenly, with Charlie dead, the spotlight had swung in her direction and she felt like a rabbit caught in the headlamps. She was worried about being found wanting.

There was a movement below her on the sand, which suddenly caught her eye. She looked down and found herself staring into the face of a young boy. He looked about seven or eight, with tousled fair hair, and a snub nose covered in freckles – a 'Just William' child, except he wasn't … there was something oddly haunting about his gaze, an almost adult look way beyond his years. Whatever his thoughts, it was certainly not about the 'Outlaws' next adventure. She stared back at him, trying to analyse what was wrong, and at the same time wondering why the child seemed oddly familiar. It was he who dropped his gaze first, nervously, shrinking away as if he wanted to be anonymous, unseen. He had been making a sandcastle, a rather complicated affair, with many turrets. A man was helping him, his father presumably. Felicity turned her attention to the man. He looked rather old to be the boy's father, but then people were having children later and later these days. He said something to the boy that Felicity could not catch but his tone sounded gentle and affectionate, and the boy jumped up, collecting his spade and bucket. The man took his hand and they began walking away from Felicity across the beach. After a few yards the boy looked back, and there it was again, that haunted look. Something wasn't right. He turned away abruptly and man and boy continued their progress across the beach, the boy's spade trailing a groove in the sand as they walked. Felicity watched them until they were no more than shadows in the growing dusk. All her instincts shouted that there was something terribly wrong with the child and then it struck her – the boy was frightened of her, of her scrutiny. But why, and why did she feel she had seen him before somewhere? She closed her eyes trying to search her mind as to why his little face was so familiar. No memory stirred. 'You're being hypersensitive because of Mel,' she told herself, turning away from the harbour. It was almost dark now. She began hurrying up the road towards Jericho Cottage, concern for her own daughter eclipsing any further thought of the child.

2

Detective Inspector Keith Penrose dropped his mobile phone onto his desk, clumsily pulled out his chair and sat down heavily. He put his head in his hands, shut his eyes and braced himself to receive the feelings which he knew were about to overwhelm him. Despite his anticipation, he was ill prepared for the avalanche of grief, misery and, most surprisingly, anger which crowded in, the pain of it making him gasp out loud. Carly, his little girl, had cancer. It was unthinkable, unbelievable. She was only twenty-six, the baby of the family. How, why? There was no history of cancer in his family, or Barbara's as far as he knew. Memories surged in – Carly a baby, pink and plump, so much easier and more placid than her brother had been, an absolute joy; Carly the toddler, walking unsteadily across the hall, arms up stretched to greet him on his return from work; Carly, the cross country runner like her father, sprinting the last few hundred yards way ahead of the rest of the field. He standing at the finishing line, bursting with pride. Carly, on

17

graduation day, Carly, Carly … The wave of anger which had been hovering broke over Keith, with such ferocity that he could feel the heat of it rising through his body. It shocked him. He was not a man used to strong emotions; there was no place for them in his job nor at home, particularly now the children had gone. Was it the state of the bloody planet that had done this to his little girl, the chemicals, the pollutants … he felt so hopeless, so powerless. Sudden tears rolled down his cheeks. He wiped them away hurriedly, afraid in case a colleague should come into his office and catch him crying, an appalling thought. Barbara, his wife, was with Carly, of course, they were at Derriford Hospital, Carly had her test results. His wife wanted Keith there, naturally, but he couldn't be, he just couldn't.

'No change there, then,' Barbara had said caustically down the telephone.

'Just let me speak to her, will you,' Keith had replied, 'I'll explain.'

'No need, no explanations necessary. Work comes first, as usual, it always has, we're both used to that, Keith.'

The body of a woman had been pulled out of the Fal earlier that morning. The new young police surgeon on the scene had confirmed what Keith could already see, that the woman was in her thirties and that she had been strangled. It was unusual for medics to commit themselves to anything at the scene although the finger marks and bruising around her neck and the face bloated by strangulation left little room for doubt. The lad would learn to be more cautious, Keith thought sagely.

'She's only been in the water a few hours,' Keith had said. It was a statement, not a question. Having spent most of his policing life in the West Country he was something of an expert on drowning.

'Not more than seven or eight, I should think,' the earnest young doctor agreed. 'I'll be able to let you know more in a few hours.'

The call had come through at two o'clock. The woman had no trace of drugs or alcohol in her system. She had died of asphyxiation, time of death indicated at between one and two am. There was no identity on her, no one had reported her missing and her DNA was currently being checked against the police database.

Keith let out a deep sigh and lay back in his chair. So where did his priorities lie so far as these two young women were concerned? One dead, strangled, a life already over, beyond help now, a stranger. The other, beautiful – at least in his eyes – clever, with an exciting future mapped out, now fighting for her life, his daughter. The fact was, there was nothing practical he could do up at Derriford. Barbara, would be in charge, even if he was there, and giving Carly all the support she needed. Here though, he could make a difference. The first few hours after a murder were the most vital, Keith believed. However callous, however pre-meditated the murder might have been, in the immediate aftermath, those responsible were often jumpy, often made mistakes, often gave themselves away by some sub-conscious slip of the tongue, inappropriate action, muddled thinking. His place was here, and he knew it, but the work versus home dilemma never ceased to be hard, and never had it been harder than today. Had there ever been a time when he put his family ahead of his job? He couldn't remember it and the thought made him desperately sad.

There was a knock on the door and a familiar head appeared.

'You alright, boss?' It was his sergeant, Jack Curnow.

'Yes, of course I'm alright,' Keith snapped. Jack frowned, coming into Keith's tiny and chaotic office, and closing the door behind him.

'Not having much luck with that body, sir. No DNA match I'm afraid and still no one has come forward to report her missing.'

'I don't think she's local,' said Keith.

'What makes you say that, boss?' Jack asked.

Keith shrugged. He stood up and hands in pockets wandered over to the window. He didn't want to meet his sergeant's eye. He didn't want him to see the hurt, the panic, the anguish that he felt must be on display for anyone to see – never mind his sergeant who knew him so well. 'I can't explain exactly,' said Keith, 'she just doesn't feel local to me, more of an up-country person.'

'That used to be something we could say,' Jack said, 'but not any more. Every town's the same now, same high street shops so the same clothes, no individuality. When you look at someone now they could come from anywhere – Redruth, Reading, Redditch, Camborne, Cardiff, Chester …' He was clearly pleased with the analogy and was warming to his theme.

Keith cut him short. 'Okay, okay. I've got the drift. We need an artist's impression, double quick, of how she would have looked in life and give it to all the local press, we'll put the story out tomorrow.' Jack didn't move. 'Well go on then, jump to it.'

'Are you sure you're alright, sir? You just seem sort of off beam, somehow.'

Keith turned, meeting Jack's eyes at last. They had been through a lot together, he was a good lad, it was hard to lie to him, it didn't feel right. 'No, not really,' he answered truthfully.

'Do you want to talk about it, sir?'

'Absolutely not.'

'Why not? A problem shared and all that.'

'Jack, just mind your own sodding business, will you.'

Jack was profoundly shocked. His boss never

swore. Regardless of how awful the circumstances that confronted them, his language was always impeccable. Keith was a master of the understatement so he used words such as distressing, inappropriate and unfortunate ... he was endlessly courteous, endlessly patient and endlessly correct – 'mind your own sodding business,' Jack could not believe his ears. Without another word he left the room.

Felicity and Mel were sitting comfortably in front of the fire in Annie Trethewey's parlour drinking mugs of tea and eating her delicious home-made rock cakes.

'I haven't had one of these for years,' said Felicity, 'my mother used to make them.'

'My mother didn't,' said Mel, her voice surprisingly bitter.

'You didn't like cake,' said Felicity, not unreasonably.

'That's not the point,' said Mel, 'other people's mothers always used to have cakes baked for them when they came home from school.'

Annie gave both mother and daughter a quizzical look, her gaze settling on Mel.

'Not much point in your mother baking you cakes after school if you didn't like them, is it my bird. Plain daft, if you ask me.'

Mel was grumpily silent in response. There was

an awkward pause. Felicity hurriedly filled the gap, glancing at the window. 'I wish this rain would let up,' she said. 'I need to go down to the pier and find a lobster pot.'

'Whatever for, Mum?' Mel asked.

'It's for my book illustrations, I'm getting horribly behind. I've tried taking some pictures of a lobster pot off the internet but I can't get the angle I want, I need to copy the real thing.'

'What on earth is the book about?' Mel asked with a studied lack of real interest.

'It's a children's book,' said Felicity, 'the main character is a seagull.'

'Blessed seagulls,' said Annie, 'I can't think why anybody wants to write about those dratted things.'

'Actually,' said Felicity, 'it's quite a sweet story. It's about this seagull who gets caught up in some fishing line and the fisherman saves her and then a few weeks later she saves the fisherman's life when his boat's capsized and he's nearly drowning – a sort of Androcles and the Lion story.'

'Sounds a bit far fetched to me,' said Mel.

'Of course it's far fetched,' said Felicity, patiently, 'it's a children's story but it's nicely told and I just want to do it justice with my illustrations.'

'I've an idea,' said Annie, 'it's going to rain like this all day. Why don't you go back to your cottage and get on with your illustrations and Mel can stay here and help me paint that little front guest room that you used to have.'

'I'd be useless,' said Mel. 'I don't know how to paint.'

'Well, it's about time you learnt, my girl. One of these days you'll have a home of your own and then you'll need to know what you're about.'

'I hope by the time I have a home of my own,' said Mel, 'I'll be able to afford to pay somebody else to paint the walls for me.'

'Mel, that's really rude!' said Felicity, shocked.

'Why?' said Mel, unrepentant. 'It's not intended to be, it's just a fact. It's one of those skills that I don't feel I'll ever need.' She stopped short seeing the stricken expression on her mother's face. She turned around to Annie. 'I'll help you though,' she said, with a ghost of a smile, 'after all, there's nothing else to do around here.'

'I'm so sorry about Mel,' said Felicity in the hall, as Annie showed her to the door.

'No need to be,' said Annie, cheerfully. 'She's suffering, poor little thing, something is really upsetting her. I'll see what I can do to sort her out, my girl, don't you fret.'

Felicity gave Annie a quick hug. 'I never need to fret when you're sorting things out, Annie. I know she couldn't be in better hands.'

'Talking of safe hands,' said Annie, opening the door. 'Did you see your inspector's got a big case again? Pulled the body of a woman out of the Fal yesterday, he was on the news last night, reckon it was murder.' She smiled cheekily. 'Still with Inspector Penrose on the case they'll soon find out what's what.'

Felicity scrutinised Annie for a moment but there was no apparent touch of irony, her words sounded genuine enough. 'A good man and a good policeman,' Felicity agreed.

'So long as there's somebody else in charge of the case,' Annie said, still smiling.

'What do you mean?' Felicity looked confused.

'You solved his last case, didn't you? He would never have managed to work out that one without you.'

Felicity laughed, stepping out into the street. It was still raining hard and she pulled the hood of her coat over her head. 'I expect he'll manage without me this time,' she called, as she set off for her cottage.

It was one of those relentlessly wet Cornish days, with just enough wind to make sure that the rain was not only falling vertically, but also coming in gusts horizontally. In seconds she was soaked. Head bowed, she turned the corner by the Sloop Inn and was hurrying towards her cottage when, quite literally, she bumped into someone. She stepped back.

'I'm so sorry, I wasn't looking where I was ...'

The words dried on her lips. It was the man and the boy from the day before.

'Quite alright,' the man said, 'my fault too, dreadful weather.'

Felicity looked down at the boy. The white blond hair was plastered to his head and he was clearly soaking, poor child, but what struck her with force was his obvious misery – his eyes were red ringed and it looked as though tears as well as rain were pouring down his cheeks. He was also still achingly familiar. Felicity dragged her eyes away from the child and stared at the man. He was pleasant enough looking, in his late fifties, early sixties, Felicity judged, thinning grey hair, kind brown eyes, slightly aqualine nose. He had the hint of a military bearing but now he seemed worn down, and like the boy, there was a sadness about him and an agitation. She opened her mouth to say something, but no words came out and within seconds they were off down Fore Street. As they trudged along the man slipped an arm around the boy's shoulders. Their shoulders were hunched in an identical way and it wasn't just against the rain. Felicity felt she could almost see the misery flowing off them. She stood, rooted to the spot as they disappeared from sight. Then the wind caught some water that had puddled in the gutter and hurled it straight over her. She gasped and turning, ran up the street to Jericho Cottage.

After a shower and a change of clothes, Felicity made a cup of tea and sat down at her desk. She picked up her pencil and tried to concentrate on the next page of drawings, but her mind kept returning to the man and boy. She tried to analyse what it was that distressed her so much about them. Their relationship seemed comfortable, the boy appeared happy in the man's company, neither threatened by him nor afraid of him in any way. The man was apparently kind to the boy, too, taking his hand and putting his arm around his shoulders, speaking to him gently. Yesterday they had not seemed sad, it was just that the boy appeared to resent her scrutiny, not resent exactly, it was more as if he was almost afraid of it. Today though, something had happened, something to make them both deeply unhappy, traumatised almost, and why, oh why was the child so familiar. Where had she seen him before? Perhaps prompted by Annie's comments, her mind strayed to Detective Inspector Keith Penrose.

Following the murder of Felicity's husband, Charlie, Keith Penrose had been instrumental in helping her unravel the mystery of his death. He had been difficult at times, inscrutable, dour, and it had taken him a long time to take her seriously but she respected him enormously, liked him too. Maybe she would go and see him and ask him to check his missing children's register. All her life Felicity had been plagued with brief episodes of second sight.

Occasionally they were very strong, like the one in which she had relived the moment her husband had been killed. At other times, they took the form of no more than shadowy feelings. She tried to analyse what she was feeling now – the little boy was in trouble, she was sure of it and if that was the case then it was her duty to do something about it.

Inspector Penrose was late the following morning, an unheard of event. He sat down heavily at his desk which, as usual, was piled high with files and random pieces of paper. The hand holding a polystyrene cup shook as he took a sip of coffee, he felt absolutely exhausted. Barbara and Carly had arrived back from Derriford at nine o'clock the previous evening. Carly had been subdued, but friendly, and wanted to do nothing more than go to bed. After she was safely upstairs Barbara had been vitriolic in her condemnation of his behaviour – it had gone on and on. While he had wanted details of Carly's treatment and prognosis, Barbara was too busy rubbishing him both as a father and a husband to explain what he so badly wanted to know. The trouble was, he knew Barbara was right.

Carly had Hodgkinson's Lymphoma, chemotherapy was to start in a week's time. Her lovely hair would fall out and she would feel sick and wretched. He couldn't bear it for her, it was a nightmare. Why Carly, why not him? He had lived most of his life, hers had only just started.

There was a tentative knock on the door. 'There's a Mrs Paradise in reception,' the young constable smiled at the name, 'she says she needs to speak to you. Shall I put her in one of the interview rooms or shall I get someone else to see her?'

'No, no, that's fine,' said Keith, 'show her in, please.'

Like a watery sun coming up from behind the clouds, Keith felt a slight rise of spirits and smiled slightly to himself. Felicity Paradise – whatever nonsense would she have dreamed up now? Still whatever it was, he didn't care, it would be good to see her again.

As usual she was eccentrically dressed in a wildly colourful Afghan coat and scarf and what appeared to be pink wellington boots. She looked good, younger than he remembered, as if a heavy burden had been lifted from her, which he supposed it had. He stood up and came around from behind his desk.

'Mrs Paradise, how good to see you.'

'And you, Inspector Penrose.' They shook hands warmly. 'I see nothing has changed in here,' she said looking pointedly at his desk.

'It's the way I work,' he said, defensively. 'I know where everything is.'

'No doubt,' she smiled again. 'I'm sorry to trouble you, I know you have a murder on your hands at the moment so I'll be brief. Do you have any missing children in the area?'

Keith removed a pile of files from a chair and Felicity sat down, Keith returning to behind his desk. 'There are always missing children,' he said, wearily.

'I mean a very young child, inspector, not a teenager. He's about seven or eight I should think, a boy, blonde hair and freckles.

Inspector Penrose let out a big sigh. 'This wouldn't by any chance be one of your little visions, would it, Mrs Paradise?'

Felicity also sighed, but in her case with exasperation. 'No it wouldn't, inspector. It's just that I've seen this man and boy a couple of times in St Ives and something's not right. When I saw them yesterday the boy was crying and they both looked so miserable, devastated almost.'

'Children do cry, Mrs Penrose.'

She had forgotten how sarcastic he could be. 'I am aware of that, inspector, only this is different.'

'Why don't you try and find them again and see if you can conjure up a vision about the child, that might help?' His voice was light, semi-joking, but his manner was annoying. He was clearly not taking the matter at all seriously.

'If only I could have my visions to order,' she said, with sudden anger. 'A sighting on 8/11 as to what was going to happen to the Twin Towers would have been helpful for a start. It is not like that, you know it isn't. Would you just check the missing persons' register for me. There is something very familiar about the boy and I just can't place it'

'I can certainly do that,' said Inspector Penrose, also clearly irritated, 'but I don't expect to find anything. There is no child of that age reported missing in the West Country, we would be searching high and low if there were.'

Felicity stood up. 'Thank you, inspector. I'm sorry to have troubled you.'

Keith stood up, he didn't want her to go yet and he regretted upsetting her. He just felt so uptight, so volatile, so overwhelmed by strong emotions he was finding it difficult to deal with because they were totally foreign to him. He tried delaying tactics. 'How have you been then, Mrs Penrose, how are you coping with your new life?' He gave her a genuinely warm smile.

She relented. 'I'm coping very well, thank you inspector, but I'm not so sure I would have been doing so well without your help.'

Keith frowned. 'How do you mean?'

'What you achieved, what we achieved together, enabled me to find – what's that truly appalling American word – closure.' Keith winced in sympathy. 'I think without finding out why Charlie died, I would have ended up in a home for the bewildered. I am in your debt, inspector, and here I am badgering you about missing children, I'm sorry.'

'That's alright,' he said, 'and how are your children?'

'Fine too, well, no that's not quite true, my son is fine but my daughter is not very good.'

'Oh?' Inspector Penrose, enquired.

'When I say not good, she's lost her job, or rather given it up. She's a lawyer like her father but she's come home and seems to be rather sad and confused about life at the moment. Daughters, much more trouble than sons, don't you find?'

At her words something in his chest began to ache and there was suddenly a lump in his throat the size of a football. 'Yes,' he managed.

Felicity realised immediately something was terribly wrong. 'Inspector, what have I said?' She put a tentative hand on his arm.

He rallied. 'No, it's nothing.'

She was not going to give up that easily. 'It is something, what's happened? What did I say to upset you?'

'My daughter, Carly, she's twenty six and she's just been diagnosed with Hodgkinson's Lymphoma.'

'Oh My God, I'm so sorry. What a completely crass thing for me to have said.' Felicity was mortified.

'You weren't to know,' said Keith.

'Even so. When did all this happen?'

'Only yesterday,' said Keith, 'or at least, that's when we had the test results. It has been hanging over us for several weeks now. She's going to have treatment and chemotherapy.' His kind grey eyes met Felicity's, he looked like a beaten child.

'What is the prognosis?' she asked, gently.

Keith had always admired her for her directness and strangely it was a relief to say the words. 'About fifty-fifty I think, at least that is what they're telling us.'

'Then focus on the fifty per cent which is going to see her well again,'

'That's what I am trying to do,' said Keith, as he ran a hand through his hair. 'Only, it was just such a shock.'

'I can imagine,' said Felicity, 'and here's me moaning about my daughter's job. I'm so sorry.'

'Well, at least my daughter has the medicine for her problems,' said Keith.

'I think my daughter may have found a medicine for hers too,' Felicity smiled.

'And what would that be?' Keith asked.

'Annie Trethewey, she's taken Mel under her wing and is making her paint one of the guest rooms.'

'Dear of her,' said Keith, smiling too, 'that girl of yours couldn't be in better hands.'

'And I'm sure that's true of yours, too,' said Felicity.

'Let's hope so,' he agreed.

3

Mother and daughter developed a very satisfactory routine over the next few days. Mel left Jericho Cottage very early each morning and spent the day with Annie. The painting project that had begun in one bedroom now seemed to encompass the whole house, and it appeared to be just what Mel needed. She was much less scratchy and was looking altogether better and less stressed.

'It's wonderful to be working at something physical, Mum and not having to think too much. My only possible criticism is Annie's choice of radio.'

'Which is?' Felicity asked, smiling.

'Radio two, of course, at full bore. She adores Wogan, laughs at every one of his jokes – it's a nightmare!'

This left the days free for Felicity to continue with her illustrations and she was making good progress. In town, she had struck up a friendship with Chris Bailey who ran a yacht chandlery in Fore Street. A funny, moody man in his early forties, Felicity judged, he had proved invaluable in loaning her bits and pieces of boating equipment to copy for her illustrations.

'I need a cleet,' she said one day, and not only did he produce one, he threaded rope in and out of it to show her how it worked to make sure her drawing was accurate.

'You are being incredibly kind,' she told him. 'I will make sure you get a copy of the book when it's finished – do you have children?'

'Not so I'd notice,' was his odd reply, but for all his strangeness and his long haired, rather scruffy appearance, he was proving a true friend.

What made his kindness all the more flattering was Chris's legendary dislike of tourists, and with no Cornish blood in her veins, Felicity was aware she could easily fit into the category of people he loved to hate.

One day, she had arrived in his shop in time to witness an ugly scene. Some poor woman had made the mistake of asking Chris whether he sold brass front door knockers.

'This is a yacht chandlers, madam, what would I be doing with bloody door knockers?' Chris had roared.

'There's no need to speak to my wife like that, mate,' said a balding little man, with a strong Birmingham accent.

'Mate! I'm not your mate and I'll speak to your wife any way I like in my shop.'

'Now look here,' the man began, rather bravely Felicity thought, given he was half Chris's size.

'Out!' Chris shouted. 'Out right now or I'll throw you out!'

The couple beat a hasty retreat.

'This probably isn't the moment to ask to borrow an anchor,' Felicity asked nervously.

Strangely, though, the face that had been suffused with rage a moment before, relaxed into a warm smile. 'No problem, got just the thing right here for you, my girl, proper job, it is.'

All part of the rich tapestry of St Ives, Felicity smiled to herself as she left Chris's shop moments later, man-handling the anchor. It was a wonder he made a living at all.

By the time mother and daughter met for supper each night they both felt satisfied from a good day's work and had plenty to say to one another. On several occasions, Felicity had tentatively raised the subject of Mel's future, but on each occasion she was stonewalled. She had decided to leave the subject well alone.

On her breaks between work, while walking on the beach or through town, Felicity had occasionally caught sight of the boy and the man, but never close to. She had heard nothing from Keith Penrose and from experience she knew that he would contact her if there was anything to report. No news meant just that, no news. She was starting to doubt herself, starting to see the whole incident as her over-active imagination at work. She was feeling particularly vulnerable at the moment, with Mel's implied criticism of her childhood never far from her thoughts, and this in turn undermined her confidence.

Her complacency changed on Saturday morning. She walked up Fore Street to buy a pasty for her lunch, having spent a happy half hour rummaging through Chris's chandlery. Mel, as usual, was spending the day with Annie and Felicity had decided she had done enough work for the week, she would take a pasty up onto the coastal path. It was a bright, clear day, cool but with little wind – a perfect day for a walk. The boy was alone, standing in the queue for pasties, one ahead of her. She shifted her position so she could watch him surreptitiously. He was waiting patiently and seemed relaxed and confident. When his turn came his voice rang out clearly. 'Two medium steak, please,' he said and handed over the money.

What disturbed Felicity today was his continued familiarity. Watching his profile now, she knew she had met him before, somewhere. She had turned this thought over in her mind many times in the last few days. Over the years she had taught art to hundreds of pupils, but if she had taught this boy, bearing in mind his age, it could only have been in the last year for she did not teach art until Year Three. As she had not taught at all since Charlie's death, the boy could never have been a pupil of hers. It was all very odd. He received the change and turned to leave. Felicity was standing in the doorway and had to move aside to let him pass. Their eyes met, she smiled and he gave her a quick smile in response which encouraged her. 'Why do I feel I know you?' she asked. 'Have we met somewhere, Oxford perhaps?'

The boy stared at her, colour draining from his face, his eyes wide with apparent horror. He clasped the pasties to his chest, pushed past her and began running off down Fore Street. Felicity stared after him. What on earth was going on? Clearly he was terrified of her, but why?

'Next please.' The girl in the pasty shop was trying to gain her attention. Felicity gave her order. 'Does that little boy come in often?' she asked.

'Fairly regular, nice little chap. Can't think why he's not at school though?'

How completely stupid, Felicity thought. Here I am having been in the school system for all these years and it never occurred to me that of course he should be at school. It's not half term for weeks yet.

Half an hour later, sitting up at Clodgy Point gazing out across the Atlantic, Felicity made a decision. The word that seemed to have terrified the child had been Oxford. She would travel up to

Oxford for the day and do some digging around. The fact that she felt she knew the child had to mean he was linked in some way to the school where she had taught. Mary Jennings, for many years headmistress of St Leonard's School in Summertown, had just retired. From visits to her old boss at home, Felicity knew that she had every school photograph on her walls going back over years. Maybe if she had a look at the most recent ones it would jog her memory. After all her years of teaching she had become good at names and faces so it did seem very odd that she couldn't place this child.

Mel did not greet the news enthusiastically. Felicity had arranged to see Mary Jennings the next afternoon and would stay the night with her friend Gilla, before returning to St Ives the following day.

'So why do you have to go off the moment I come down to see you?' Mel asked.

'It's just one night,' Felicity said, patiently. 'I just need to check out something.'

'What?' Mel demanded.

'If I tell you, you'll think I'm silly. Let me do the checking first and then I'll tell you when I come back.'

From the robust, confident, talented head that Felicity remembered, Mary had become a rather sad figure – stooped, grey haired and somehow diminished. Her husband had died several years before her retirement, her children had all fled the nest and she seemed to be rattling about in the big old family home in Headington. Clearly she was delighted to see Felicity and showed her through into a sunny conservatory where they drank coffee and gossiped for some time. At last they got down to business.

'So,' said Mary, 'tell me what you are looking for?'

'A little boy, very blonde, freckles, snub nose, nice looking little chap of about seven or eight perhaps, at the most. I don't think I ever taught him, but I know him, and the only connection I can think of is with the school.'

'You could have only taught him in the last year,' some of the sharpness was back, 'when you were no longer at school. Maybe you just recognised him from the playground.'

'It's possible,' Felicity agreed, 'I feel there is a school connection. What I was hoping is that I could just look through the photographs of the last few years.'

'What is your interest in the child?' Mary asked, clearly intrigued.

'I don't know,' said Felicity, 'that's the stupid part. He is staying in St Ives at the moment, with a man who could be his father or perhaps his grandfather. The child seems unhappy and frightened and, of course, he should be in school.'

Mary looked up sharply. 'Have you informed the police, I suppose in today's awful world, the man could be a paedophile.'

'Yes, I have informed the police but they have no missing children in the area. Somehow, though, I don't suspect there's anything wrong with the relationship between the man and the boy. I can't tell you why, but there is something about the child which worries me, and of course, I find his familiarality very disconcerting.'

'Let's see if we can find him then,' said Mary, getting up stiffly.

They laid a green baize cloth on her mahogany dining room table and Mary lifted down the previous six years of school photographs.

'The youngest he could have been when he joined the school is three as you know but let's be on the safe side and cover the last six years.' she said, 'I'll fetch you a magnifying glass and then I'll leave you alone to concentrate.'

Felicity went through each photograph in turn. She didn't waste time with the senior girls at the top of the photograph, she concentrated on the infants, painstakingly checking each face.

Half an hour later, with a sigh, she completed the sixth photograph. She couldn't find him, he wasn't there.

'Any luck?' Mary called.

'None, I'm afraid,' said Felicity, 'shall I hang

these back up for you.'

'That would be kind. I'll put on the kettle.'

With a heavy heart Felicity began hanging the photographs. It had been a complete wild goose chase and she had upset Mel in the process. It was as she replaced the oldest photograph for the Year 1998 that Felicity's eyes strayed to a young girl in the back row of perhaps ten or eleven. She had fair hair, very fair, a snub nose and freckles.

Felicity was on school home-time duty, standing by the gate saying goodbye to the pupils and hello to the parents collecting them. A car had screeched to a halt on the zigzag line in front of the school gate. She had walked over quickly to ask for it to be moved. A blonde woman climbed out of the car and stumbled unsteadily. 'Won't be a tick,' she said to Felicity, 'I'm just picking up my daughter.'

'You can't park here, it's dangerous,' said Felicity.

'I'll do what I bloody well like,' the woman retorted, 'bearing in mind the enormous school fees we have to pay.' She barged past Felicity, appearing to have difficultly walking straight. 'Megan, Megan, where are you?' She called. Her voice was slurred.

A little girl detached herself from a group of children. She looked both embarrassed and shocked. 'Mum, what are you doing here?'

'I've come to pick you up, darling. I've got

42

George in the car.'

'We can't go with you, Mum, Dad will be here in a minute.'

'You come along with me right now young lady.' The woman grabbed the child's arm, none to gently. Megan tried to pull away.

Felicity rushed over. 'Excuse me,' she said, 'Megan, is this lady your mother?' Megan nodded dumbly. 'And is she supposed to be picking you up?' Megan shook her head.

'Of course I'm supposed to be picking her up. You heard, she's my daughter. You just stay out of it, you stupid cow.'

Much to her astonishment the woman gave Felicity a hearty thump in the chest, sending her reeling backwards, falling into an ungainly heap and bruising both her bottom and her dignity. Grabbing the child, the woman was back in the car before Felicity had scrambled to her feet. She ran over and tried to open the passenger door of the car. Megan was in the front staring out, white faced. The woman was fumbling with the keys, trying to start the engine. Felicity couldn't open the passenger door, so she tried the back door, peering through the window, wrenching at the handle. A face stared back. It was that of a small boy strapped into a car seat. Felicity had found the boy from St Ives.

'Are you alright, dear?' The voice came from a

long way away. Felicity turned to see Mary Jennings standing beside her. She had an arm round her and looked deeply concerned. 'I couldn't reach you, you seemed to have blanked out. I wondered if you were starting a fit or something.'

'No, no, I'm alright,' said Felicity. 'Could I just sit down for a moment.'

'A glass of water?'

'Yes, please.' Felicity tried to marshall her thoughts. 'Mary, this is all about the Hope family. I should have known.'

Mary placed the water in front of her. 'Please don't do this to yourself, Felicity. What else could you have done? We've been through it so many times, you were completely exonerated both by the court and by the governors. You did your very best to stop her.'

'The boy, I've been searching for, Mary, the boy from St Ives, it's George Hope.'

Felicity was due at her friend Gilla's house for supper. She had said she expected to be there by five. It was now half past six and she was still sitting on a bench in the Parks with no apparent ability to move, watching the River Cherwell flow by.

It had been the only blot on her career, the only time when she had seriously wondered whether she should be teaching. Megan and George Hope's mother was a drunk. Their father, Philip, was in business of some sort, a very successful, dynamic man, by all accounts. When his wife Lizzie had started drinking night and day and failing to look after their children properly, he had taken very firm action. He had removed them from the family home, set up a new home for them and fought successfully for custody. On the day Lizzie Hope came to collect Megan, it emerged that she had been drinking steadily all day. After an abusive encounter at George's nursery school, she had succeeded in snatching him and getting him into her car. The school had telephoned the police immediately but it had not been in time to stop her collecting Megan as well. On leaving St Leonard's, Lizzie had headed for the Oxford ring road where she had crashed the car into an oncoming lorry. George was completely unhurt, Lizzie had broken a leg and several fractured ribs. Megan had been killed outright.

For years the incident had haunted Felicity, it still did. What surprised her was that George's face had not been instantly recognisable. She supposed she had buried the whole terrible incident so deeply that she couldn't immediately recall it. Philip Hope had accused the school of negligence and in Felicity's view he had been right to do so. However, the court was completely satisfied that Felicity had done her best. There had been plenty of witnesses – mothers, pupils and the young student teacher who had been coaching netball and on hearing the commotion had come running over … also too late to stop the car. Charlie's partner Josh Buchanan had represented Felicity in court. There was no case against Felicity to be heard the judge announced. George was returned to his father's custody with occasional limited and supervised access to his mother, once she was recovered and served a largely suspended sentence for the manslaughter of her daughter.

'Megan,' Felicity said the name aloud to no one in particular. The child she had failed to save, the child she should have been able to protect.

It was some while before Felicity was able to lift her tortured thoughts from the past and consider the present. What on earth was George doing in St Ives and who was the man with him? It certainly wasn't his father, Philip, he was much too old. How could she be so certain it was George, after all he had been little more than a baby when she had seen him last? Was the horror of the Hope's accident playing tricks on her mind which seemed to be doing somersaults to try and make sense of it all.

A couple of little girls in High School uniform were walking along the path in front of her, chattering. They reminded her of Mel at the same age.

'What am I doing?' she thought. 'My daughter is down in St Ives because she needs me and I'm up here doing what – trying to make peace with the past?' Stiffly she stood up and shivered. Gilla would know what to do.

Gilla Townsend had been Felicity's best friend since they were at school together. Wacky, eccentric, opinionated and larger than life, Gilla was nonetheless a true and loyal friend. She took one look at the bedraggled figure on her doorstep and swept her into a huge hug.

'Oh, Fizzy,' was all she said and without another word led her friend through to the Aga, sat her on a chair in front of it and poured an enormous glass of red wine. Gilla sat down at the kitchen table and studied Felicity in silence for a moment. 'I knew you should never have moved to St Ives. You need to be here with your friends. You're in a frightful state, what on earth has happened?'

Five years ago the Hope case had been big news in Oxford and, as Felicity's friend, there was no detail of it with which Gilla was not familiar. They had been over it a thousand times. Felicity quickly filled in the details of her day.

'So what do you think?' she said, turning enormous anxious eyes on Gilla.

'Your mind is playing tricks on you,' said Gilla, firmly, 'you're so isolated down there, down in Cornwall, and it is not surprising that your past comes back to haunt you in one way or another. Of all the things that have happened to you in your life, Megan's death is the biggest trauma you have had to cope with next to Charlie's death. You are simply torturing yourself. You need to come home to Oxford, Fizzy, you really do.'

'I'm not all alone in St Ives,' said Felicity, 'I've got Mel with me at the moment.' Another long explanation ensued while Mel's dilemma was explained. The wine sunk lower in the bottle.

'There are any number of fair haired, snub nosed, freckled little boys in the world,' said Gilla, 'and I don't see how you could possibly recognise George as he is today. He must have been two, at the most three, at the time of the accident and you only saw him the once. Children's faces change so much during that period.'

'Some do,' Felicity acknowledged, 'but not this one. At least,' she rubbed a weary hand across her forehead, 'at least I don't think so. I'm starting to confuse myself now. I sort of re-saw the whole thing at Mary's this afternoon, you know how it is.' Gilla did indeed know. She was a veteran observer of what she called 'Fizzy's little moments'.

Gilla, a slapdash but inventive cook, threw together a delicious paella in what seemed a matter of moments. 'Ellie is sorry to miss you,' she said, 'but she's at a sleepover with some friends tonight.'

Ellie was Gilla's daughter and Felicity's goddaughter. 'I'm sorry to miss her too,' said Felicity, 'but a sleepover suggests that she is making more friends than she used to.'

48

'She certainly is,' said Gilla, 'she's been a different girl since she came back from her holiday in Cornwall this summer. Your Annie is a real miracle worker.'

'I'm hoping she is going to do the same for Mel,' Felicity replied, ruefully.

The following morning Felicity left early for her long journey back to Cornwall.

'So what are you going to do about this little boy?' Gilla asked.

'Nothing,' said Felicity, firmly. 'You're right, I must have been mistaken. My mind was playing tricks. George has to be living somewhere with his father, the boy I saw must be someone else altogether.'

'Excellent,' said Gilla, hugging her, 'now will you promise to reconsider making your life in St Ives.'

'I have reconsidered,' said Felicity, 'and the answer is I'm staying put, but bless you for wanting me back.'

However, instead of taking the A420 to Swindon en route to the M4, Felicity drove straight into central Oxford to the offices of Buchanan and Simms, formally Paradise, Buchanan and Simms, to talk to Josh Buchanan about the Hope case.

The receptionist was new since Charlie's time,

something which threw Felicity completely. Such a small thing really but it showed how time had moved on and changed in just the year since Charlie had died.

'I'd like to see Josh Buchanan, please,' she said.

'I'm sorry. I'm afraid he's booked up all morning.' The girl barely glanced up from the newspaper she was reading.

'He'll see me,' said Felicity, firmly.

'I can't disturb him at the moment, he's with a client.'

The mulish girl, a bottle blonde in her early twenties, was clearly enjoying being obstructive. She could hardly be good for business. The unworthy thought that she was probably only in the job because she was granting Josh sexual favours crept into Felicity's mind and made her smile. Josh was a notorious womaniser and this brash, large bosomed girl was just his type.

'Just slip him a note,' Felicity said, patiently, 'you'll be in trouble if you don't.'

'I don't like being threatened,' the girl replied angrily. Charlie would have had a fit if they'd employed this girl in his day.

'I'm not going to make a fuss,' said Felicity, 'but I can assure you that Josh will be less than pleased if you don't inform him that I'm here.'

Reluctantly the girl reached for a pen and paper. 'Can I have your name?'

'Felicity Paradise.'

It was extraordinary that the name meant nothing to her, that in just over a year the memory of Charlie Paradise had been expunged so thoroughly from his own kingdom as to be unrecognisable to a member of staff.

The girl returned in seconds. 'Mr Buchanan will be out in a moment,' she said, sulkily, and indeed he was, ushering a rather bewildered client out of the door.

'Fizzy!' Josh swept her into a warm embrace. 'How are you, you look wonderful.'

'Fine, fine,' Felicity lied, routinely. She studied Josh as she spoke. He was still a strikingly good looking man, tall with dark hair only slightly streaked with grey. For a dark haired person, he had the unusual combination of bright blue eyes which made his appearance even more arresting. However, he had aged and was clearly trying too hard to remain the flamboyant young man about town which was sadly no longer possible. His hair was slightly overlong, his tie juvenile and for the first time Felicity saw him as a slightly pathetic figure.

'Come into the office. What would you like – tea, coffee?'

'Coffee would be good,' said Felicity.

'Two coffees, please Fiona,' he called out to the receptionist over his shoulder, who Felicity imagined must truly hate her by now.

'So what's with this Fiona?' Felicity asked as soon as they were seated at Josh's desk.

'What do you mean?' Josh asked.

'She's terrible, Josh, very rude to potential clients, certainly she was very rude to me. I assume she must be your latest conquest.'

'Absolutely not,' said Josh, a little too quickly, 'she's young enough to be my daughter.'

'I agree,' Felicity replied, 'but I can't remember when that ever stopped you.'

'Now, now,' said Josh, 'no need to be bitchy, darling.' His voice was light but there was an edge to it. The coffee arrived and it gave Felicity a chance to consider what she was going to say. She and Josh had not met for many months, not since he had disclosed to her that there were elements of her husband's past that he should have told her about and never had. The trust was broken between them and so indeed was the depth of friendship. They would never get back to where they had been when Charlie was alive; the easy intimacy was gone forever but at this moment, there was no one else she would turn to.

'So,' said Josh, turning his prize smile on Felicity as soon as the door was closed. 'Is this a social call? It is very nice to see you after all this time.'

'No it's not, Josh,' said Felicity. She reached for her mug and took a sip of coffee. Even thinking about the Hope case made her feel sick and lightheaded. 'I've come to see you about the Hope case.'

There was a slight pause. 'Oh Fizzy,' said Josh, 'why on earth bring that up again?'

She ignored him. 'Have you the slightest idea what happened to father and son after the accident?'

'No, I haven't,' Josh said, 'as you know the mother was given a suspended sentence which was more lenient than she deserved. The father said rather unwisely in court, that he would kill her if she ever came anywhere near the boy again and this outburst, of course, had the opposite of the desired effect and goaded the judge into giving the mother supervised access. Presumably he and … what was the child's name'

'George,' said Felicity.

'… he and George started over?'

'Josh, could you find out what's happened to them for me?'

'I could,' said Josh, 'yes of course I could, but first of all I'd like to know why? You went through enough during that period, Fizzy, what on earth is the point of opening old wounds?'

'Because I think I've seen him, Josh.'

'Seen who?'

'George.'

'Where? In St Ives?'

Felicity nodded.

'Well, that's not particularly surprising, is it? I mean, heaven knows how many thousands of people visit St Ives every year.'

'He wasn't with his father, Josh. He was with some other man and he was frightened. On one day I saw him he was crying.'

Josh frowned and stared hard at Felicity. He had not lied, she did look well, better than she had done since before her husband was murdered. She still had her summer tan, her blonde hair was streaked by the sun. She had lost weight and she looked fit and years younger than her true age which must be now, he calculated, forty-seven. She didn't look like somebody who would deliberately put herself on the rack. What on earth could all this be about?

'Fizzy, the Hope case was…' he thought for a moment, 'five years ago. I don't see how you could possibly recognise George if you saw him again after all this time. It must just be a boy who looks like him.'

'That's what Gilla said.'

'Then Gilla is quite right for once,' said Josh.

'I still want you to check it out for me, Josh, I mean it. This is really important to me. I'll have no peace until I know. You tell me George is safely with his father somewhere and I will stop fussing, I promise.'

Josh smiled. 'All right, if that's what it takes to bring you peace of mind then of course I'll do it.' He made a note on his pad. 'Now tell me, how are the family?'

'Jamie is fine,' said Felicity with a smile, 'but I'm

54

having trouble with Mel.'

'Mel? Why on earth are you having trouble with Mel?' Josh's brow knitted.

'She's been passed over for the tenancy and she's in such a huff that she's resigned. She's back in St Ives with me, jobless at the moment, bewildered and she can't understand why it happened.

Josh's frown deepened. 'You mean Michael Ferguson didn't take her on?'

'No, he didn't,' said Felicity. 'Do you know him?'

'Yes, I do. I was at university with his older brother who is also a barrister. I used to stay with the family sometimes, they own a huge pile out in Gloucestershire, nice people actually.'

'So if you know Michael can you think of any reason on earth why he should pass over Mel for some chinless wonder called Jeremy who appears to have nothing about him at all and is a complete 'yes man'?'

'No I can't,' Josh answered. 'I can't imagine.'

'Well, if you ever bump into him I would be grateful if you could find out something of the background. It's a complete mystery to me and much more importantly, to Mel.'

'Oh, I doubt if I will see him in the foreseeable future,' Josh said a little hurriedly, 'we did bump into one another a few months ago and at a family do, but before that I hadn't seen him for years.'

'Then, I'll just leave the thought with you,' said Felicity. 'Remember, Mel is you goddaughter.' She stood up to go. 'It's been nice seeing you Josh. I'd better go, I've got a long journey home.'

'You're going back to St Ives now?'

Felicity nodded.

'I wish you didn't live so far away, Fizzy.'

'That's what everyone says, but it suits me.' She kissed him on the cheek and started towards the door. 'There is just one other thing Josh. You presumably could lay your hands on the Hope file relatively easily.'

Josh nodded. 'Yes, of course I can. Why?'

'Could you see if you can find a summary of the case – a newspaper cutting would do or maybe some notes of your own, a few details anyway. If so, would you send them to Inspector Penrose in Truro.'

Josh gave a short laugh. 'Inspector Penrose, you haven't involved that poor devil again, have you?'

'I'm afraid so,' said Felicity, 'but I feel bad about it, he has a murder on his hands at the moment, which is more than enough to cope with without me badgering him.'

'I agree – he has my deepest sympathy,' said Josh.

Felicity smiled. 'Thanks a bunch, I'll pass it on.'

4

Felicity came back into the kitchen having answered the telephone, during a rather shamefully late breakfast that she and Mel were sharing, two days after her return from Oxford.

'I have a red hot date with a policeman,' she announced.

Mel looked up. 'Really, when?'

'Today at lunchtime. That's alright with you, is it?'

'Yes, I'll be painting as usual. Who's the date, Mum?'

'Inspector Penrose. He was the policeman who was so helpful with Dad's case. He's in St Ives and has asked me to have lunch with him at Porthminster Beach Café.'

'Heavens, that sounds fun,' said Mel.

'Actually,' said Felicity, 'the invitation wasn't couched in very flattering terms. He said he was going to be in St Ives anyway, he supposed he'd have to eat and would I care to join him as there were things he needed to discuss and it would be a good use of his time.'

Mel laughed. 'Well your inspector knows how to make a girl feel special.'

Felicity regarded her daughter in silence for a moment. 'You know Mel, it's about time someone made you feel special.'

'That, if I may say so Mum, is a typical mother's remark.' Mel was immediately defensive.

'I'm sure you're right,' said Felicity, 'but so am I. What has been lacking from your life for some long time, Mel, is fun.'

Mel stood up abruptly. 'A lecture I don't need. I'm off to Annie's. Have a good time with your inspector.'

Within seconds she was out of the house, shutting the front door none too quietly behind her. Felicity sighed and began clearing up the breakfast things. In the two weeks since Mel had been with her, in some respects her daughter had improved. She was calm, she spent most of every day with Annie painting, taking the odd break for a long cliff walk with the result that she looked much healthier than when she had arrived with colour in her cheeks. In some respects, their relationship was easier than it had ever been, provided that they spoke only of banalaties. The moment Felicity made any sort of remark about the future Mel walked out on her, just as she had done now.

The other aspect concerning Mel which

worried Felicity was the feeling that her daughter might be settling into a depression. Being around Mel had always been exhilarating, if exhausting; Mel had only ever had one speed and that was flat out. Now being with Mel, instead of like being in the centre of a whirlpool, was strangely calm. Annie was reassuring on the subject, insisting that it was a necessary part of both Mel's grieving and recovery, but as much as Felicity respected Annie and her views, Annie did not know her daughter as she did. She was behaving so out of character.

She finished putting the cereal bowls in the dishwasher and wandered out through her kitchen onto the balcony. St Ives was already bustling. It was a beautiful day, too good to be inside. She would take her sketchbook down to the harbour. She hoped Mel would spend some time outside today and suspected that Annie would shoo her out for a long lunch. Lunch made her think of Inspector Penrose. She imagined he might want to see her about the Hope case, details of which presumably Josh would have sent him by now. She felt suddenly shy. The Hope family and their tragedy represented the skeleton in Felicity's cupboard and she knew she would take the guilt to her grave. Since her return from Oxford, she had started to wonder whether her flight to St Ives had been as much about a fresh start away from the Hope scandal as it was about a fresh start as a widow. The scene she had played a thousand times, the point at which she could have grabbed Megan and in doing so saved her life, was lodged at the very core of her. Felicity suspected that the incident and its terrible consequences was the yardstick by which she judged everything.

It was strange that Inspector Penrose had asked her to join him for lunch, but she was grateful for the invitation. There had been no word from Josh concerning George and his whereabouts. She toyed with the idea of telephoning him, using the excuse of lunch with Inspector Penrose as the reason for knowing if he yet had a result. However, he had her mobile number. No doubt if he had anything to report she would hear during the morning.

Porthminster beach has to be one of the most beautiful places in the country, Felicity thought, as she walked across the sand to the café. Although it was September there was little hint of Autumn today. The sea was a bright azure blue, the sand white and the warmth of the sun felt more like summer. She was early so she sauntered along the edge of the sea, only cutting up across the beach when she was opposite the square white beach café building. She was surprised that Inspector Penrose was already there sitting at a table outside.

He stood up as she came onto the terrace. 'I hope this is alright for you, Mrs Paradise,' he said, 'only I spend so much of my life in a stuffy office, it's good to be outside and such a bonus to have this weather in September.'

'It's perfect, inspector and very kind of you.'

They ordered wine and some bread and sat in contented silence for a few moments, gazing out across the beach towards the harbour. 'There can be few sights better than this,' Keith said after a pause.

'Venice?' Felicity ventured.

'I'm a Cornishman,' said Keith, with a smile. 'Foreign parts are alright in short bursts, but there's nowhere like Cornwall, and nowhere in Cornwall like St Ives on a day like this,' he smiled, 'Not that I've ever been to Venice.'

'It's a very special place,' said Felicity, 'maybe you should save it for your retirement.'

'I try not to think about retirement,' said Keith, 'I just can't imagine it.'

It was an odd remark, Felicity thought as their wine was served. She supposed being a policeman at his level was so all consuming it was probably very difficult to split the man from the job. She said as much.

'I can't argue,' Keith replied, 'and my wife would certainly agree with you.' They ordered their food and Keith gave Felicity a slightly quizzical look. 'The Hope case, it must have been terrible for you,' he said gently.

'Josh sent you the file then?' Felicity could not meet his eye and played with her fork, head bent.

'Yes, he did, but I'm not quite sure why.'

'Didn't he tell you that I believe the boy I keep seeing in St Ives is George Hope, the surviving child.'

'Yes, he did,' said Inspector Penrose, 'so immediately I checked the missing person's register and George Hope isn't on it. I can't imagine if a father has lost one child, he would be careless enough to lose a second without reporting the matter to the police.'

'I'm sure it's George,' said Felicity quietly, still staring at the table.

'I think your mind is playing tricks on you Mrs Paradise, if I may say so.' The voice was kind despite the harshness of the words.

'That's what everyone thinks,' said Felicity.

'And I think in this instance everyone, whoever they may be, are right. The boy looks how you imagine George Hope would look today. God knows, I'm no psychiatrist, but by trying to 'save him' from this man he is with, you may be making a kind of subconscious attempt to right the wrongs, help the Hope family in a way you were not able to help them last time.'

At last Felicity was able to meet his gaze which was kind and compassionate – much less abrasive than the Inspector Penrose she was used to. It was reassuring. 'What you say makes complete sense, inspector and I know what I am saying sounds irrational, but I'm just sure that child is George Hope. I recognised him immediately, I just couldn't place him, I suppose because I had air-brushed the image of him out of my mind in order to cope with it all.'

'And I imagine it came back to you in one of your little visions.' Inspector Penrose smiled.

'As a matter of fact it did, but before you start ridiculing me and my visions, maybe I should remind you that they proved quite useful in the search for my husband's killer.'

'I can't argue with that,' Keith agreed, 'even if I don't understand it ... or you sometimes.' He grinned and then the smile faded. 'It must have been a terrible experience, Mrs Paradise, and I appreciate it can't have been easy for you to share this whole incident with me.'

'You're right,' said Felicity, 'and therefore maybe that will help you understand how strongly I feel about it. It is my nemesis. If I could re-run any part of my life, that thirty seconds during which Megan's mother bundled her daughter into the car is the thirty seconds I would choose. I can't bear the thought of dragging it all up again, inspector, I really can't, but nor can I let the matter drop.

Keith sighed. 'I don't know what else you expect me to do, Mrs Paradise? It appears George Hope is not missing. We don't know the boy is George Hope and we don't know that there is anything wrong or suspicious about the child in any event. You say you saw him crying and upset one day, well children do cry and do get upset. I've asked the boys who cover St Ives to look out for the child but other than that I don't see what I can do.'

'I've asked Josh Buchanan to trace George and his father to make sure they are together and alright,' said Felicity. 'Assuming he finds them, then I will be able to concede that you were all right and it is a case of mistaken identity. In which case I am very sorry indeed for wasting police time, particularly when you are so busy.'

'Having lunch on such a beautiful day here at Porthminster with such agreeable company goes a long way to redressing the balance,' Keith said gallantly.

'Thank you inspector, this is a real treat.' She hesitated. 'I think we've talked enough about me and my troubles. How about you and yours?' She saw a look of pain cross his face. 'Unless, of course, you'd rather not talk about it,' she added hurriedly.

'No,' he took a sip of wine, 'no, I rather think I would like to talk about it, except that I don't know what to say, or where to start.'

'Tell me about Carly,' Felicity asked.

'Just an ordinary girl, really,' he gazed out across the sand towards the sea.

'But not to you,' said Felicity.

He turned and smiled at her. 'No, not to me,' he

hesitated, 'she's done rather well actually. She wasn't particularly academic at school but she's always been very good at sport, loved it. I was a bit of a runner in my time and she loves to run as well. She is very good, ran at national level as a child.'

Felicity smiled gently. 'So you were a runner, were you, inspector?'

'Yes,' he said, catching her mood. 'Cross-country running was my forte, both as a boy and then later in the force. With a job like mine, it's a good skill to master. Being quick on my feet has got me out of a few scrapes over the years, I can tell you, and helped me catch a few villains, too.' He raised an eyebrow. 'I'm not quite as quick as I was though.'

'Does Carly still play sport?' Felicity asked.

Keith nodded. 'She went to Bath Spa University and read sports science and now she teaches it. She is also a coach for one of the West of England girls' cross country teams. She's very dedicated and very good, I think,' he shook his head, 'though what this illness is going to do to her career, I dread to imagine.'

'Surely they'll keep her job open for her, won't they?' Felicity asked.

'Certainly they are at the moment, but how long is it going to be before she is fit enough to work? I wish now she had some sort of desk job so she could still work and keep her mind occupied, but her treatment is going to be sufficiently debilitating that there's no way she will be able to go back to her old job for a long while.'

'Couldn't you find her some sort of temporary work at the station?' Felicity asked.

'I don't mind admitting I'd thought of that but it's just not possible these days. With budgets and all that, they don't just take on anyone.'

'She's not anyone,' said Felicity, 'she's your daughter.'

'Still,' Keith sighed. 'Anyway, I don't think she's up to any sort of job at the moment.'

'Is she finding the treatment hard?' Felicity asked.

'No, not yet, it's only just started but I can tell she's depressed and anxious and it's so out of character. She's always been, I don't know, on top of everything. I'm not saying she was born with the silver spoon. Barbara and I have never had much and I've been a fairly indifferent father, away so much because of my job. Somehow, though, for Carly, life's always landed …' he searched for words, 'butter side up. She's one of those people who makes friends easily and while she might not be brilliant at anything, she's good at most things. She's laid back without being lazy, always happy, joking, good fun I suppose but in an old fashioned way. We've never had any problems with her so far as drink or drugs are concerned.'

'Has she a boyfriend?' Felicity asked.

'Did have up to about six months ago. To be honest I didn't rate him but you know what they're like, you can't say anything, so I kept quiet. I wasn't sorry when it broke up.'

'Why did it?' Felicity asked.

'I don't know really. She said something about the relationship going nowhere. She didn't seem unduly upset at the time, I got the impression it was she who finished it.'

'Still, it means she has no one special in her life just now,' Felicity said.

'She's got her family,' Keith said, defensively. 'I'd have thought we were the best people to take her through this.'

Felicity remained silent. Through the tragedies in her own life, she had learnt that the most unexpected relationships could prove the most comforting in moments of crisis and that sometimes the sharing of pain with immediate family placed too much of a burden on them and you. Instinctively, though she felt this wasn't an appropriate thought to share just at that moment. 'You've other children, haven't you?' Felicity asked.

'Yes, a son Billy, he is a couple of years older than Carly.'

'Are they close?'

'Not really,' Keith hesitated, 'and they never were especially close, even as children. Billy is a restless sort of boy, he's in the army now doing very well, in Bosnia as a matter of fact. It's sad he can't be with us just now but compassionate leave doesn't stretch to sisters.'

By the time Felicity had walked back along the length of the beach, she realised she had come to know more about Inspector Penrose in the last hour than she had discovered in any of their previous encounters. He was a more complex man than she had realised, feelings running far deeper than the bluff policeman exterior. He had clearly been moved by the story of the Hope family and she believed him when he said he had done everything possible to check out George Hope. Certainly on the face of it, if George Hope had not been reported missing then logically George Hope wasn't missing. She was surprised not to have heard from Josh who, despite his many less attractive characteristics, was efficient and surprisingly speedy for a lawyer. Maybe there would be a message for her at home.

There was no message from Josh and that evening, Felicity found herself restless and unable to settle into her work properly. Mel had rung to say she and Annie were working late and she would grab a snack later. Felicity ranged about the cottage and then noticed the walking boots by the front door. She and Mel had been for a big hike the previous day and the boots were coated in mud. Cleaning them would be a satisfactory job to keep her occupied. She carried the two pairs of boots into the kitchen and put them in the sink. She glanced at her watch, just after six pm, time for the news while she worked. She turned on the television.

After the normal horrors of the national news, BBC Spotlight began. The top local story was of the woman's body found in the Fal the previous week. The face that stared out at Felicity from the television screen, made her gasp aloud. It was an artist's impression of the victim and as Felicity stared at the face, her stomach began to churn, she felt faint and groping behind her, found a kitchen chair and sat down heavily upon it.

The police, the voice-over assured her, were no closer to establishing the identity of the woman's body but Felicity knew exactly who she was. Felicity knew that the woman was George Hope's mother, Lizzie.

5

Josh felt foolish. He was also blaming Felicity for what he anticipated to be little more than a wild goose chase. The problem was, he could see no other way of handling a tricky situation. It had been easy enough to locate the Hope family home, Mulberry House, for father and son had not moved since the accident. When his telephone calls had received no response, he had driven out to Charlbury and found without any difficulty the delightful Georgian town house close to the church. A chat to a cooperative next door neighbour had established that the family were away. Philip Hope was abroad on business apparently and George was staying with his maternal grandparents somewhere near Bath. Tom and Clara Gresham were easy to find. Their daughter, Lizzie, had lived with them in the weeks between her being discharged from hospital and being tried for manslaughter. A quick dip into his files had established that they lived at Juniper Farmhouse on the outskirts of a village called Grittleton a few miles outside Bath. A call to the local pub had established

70

they were still there.

So here he was, driving through the delightful Somerset countryside on a glorious golden day trying to work out what on earth he should say to the Greshams to explain his visit and establish the whereabouts of George. A visit to the same pub had equipped him with directions. He had to be less than a mile from their farmhouse yet still could not begin to imagine how to tackle such a delicate subject. For all he knew, the Greshams might well blame Felicity for their granddaughter's death. He tried to remember them. He knew they had attended the court hearing in which Philip Hope had tried to bring a case against Felicity for negligence. The case had been dismissed, the judge accusing all concerned of wasting court time and causing Mrs Paradise unnecessary stress. Philip had exploded with rage, very loudly and publicly, and had therefore somewhat hijacked the whole proceedings. The Greshams had made no impact on his consciousness at all.

At a bend in the road Josh saw the gates of Juniper Farm and with a sigh, swung his gleaming Mercedes down the short tree-lined drive and into the parking area of what proved to be a delightful stone farmhouse. As soon as he stepped out of his car, there was the sound of barking dogs and two chocolate labradors careered around the side of the house, full of enthusiasm and excitement at the prospect of a visitor – guard dogs, they weren't. Josh bent to make a fuss of them which was much appreciated but with all the noise, he did not hear the front door open.

'Can I help you?' A clipped upper class English voice, a tall elegant figure – this was clearly Clara Gresham and equally clearly Josh recognised immediately that he could do nothing but tell her the exact reason for his visit. She was far too formidable.

Fighting his way past his newly acquired four-legged friends, he extended a hand which was not taken. 'My name is Josh Buchanan, I'm a solicitor.' Awkwardly he dropped his hand and fumbled about in his pocket for a business card which he handed to her. She looked at the card.

'From Oxford,' she said, as if it was an accusation.

He nodded. She studied him in silence for a moment. She was obviously in her sixties, had to be with a daughter of Lizzie's age. She was a strikingly good-looking woman and must have been beautiful once, high cheekbones, huge deep blue eyes, her white hair piled up in a neat French pleat.

'Could I trouble you for a few minutes?' Josh said, 'I just wanted to ask about your grandson.'

'George? Is anything wrong, is he hurt?' She looked and sounded frantic in an instant.

'No, no,' said Josh, 'I'm terribly sorry, I didn't

72

mean to startle you. No nothing's wrong at all, it was just … well could I come inside and I'll explain.'

He was shown through a large sunny hall into a little morning room. Clara Gresham now obviously anxious and concerned, showed him impatiently to a chair. 'So what's this about, Mr Buchanan?' She asked.

Josh explained that he represented Felicity and outlined her concerns about having thought she'd spotted George in St Ives, in a state of some distress and with a stranger. Clara listened in silence until he had finished. His story sounded ludicrous even to his own ears. 'So,' he concluded, 'I've been trying to locate George for Mrs Paradise just to establish that he's alright.'

'What an extraordinary thing,' said Clara, 'I can't understand why she imagined she would even recognise George after all this time. How the mind plays tricks.'

'I suppose so,' said Josh, 'so George isn't in St Ives?'

'No, of course he's not,' said Clara.

'He's here?' Josh asked.

'No, he's not here either,' Clara's voice was unsteady and impatient. 'George is with his father.'

'But his father is abroad on business,' Josh said.

'I'm well aware of that,' said Clara, clearly increasingly agitated, 'and George is with him.'

'It seems rather odd,' said Josh, 'bearing in mind

that it's term time and hardly much fun for a young boy.'

'Are you a father, Mr Buchanan?' Clara asked.

Josh shook his head. 'No, unfortunately not.'

'Then I should restrict your judgement on such matters until such time as you are. Philip is a single parent to all intents and purposes. He and George have had to make many adjustments over the last five years and because Philip has a demanding business, he doesn't see his son as much as he would like. George is only a little boy and it certainly isn't going to upset his schooling to miss a week or two at this stage of his career, whereas time with his father is all important.' She sighed. 'I don't know why I'm explaining all this to you, Mr Buchanan, because it really is none of your business.'

'I suppose it's understandable,' Josh persisted, 'that you should be angry with my client.'

'With Mrs Paradise?' Clara looked surprised. 'No, of course I'm not angry with her, other than her being the cause of your intrusion now. Mrs Paradise did the very best she could to prevent ...,' she hesitated, '... the tragedy, but it really is time she put the accident behind her, and moved on. Even we've had to do that so Mrs Paradise should be able to do so too.' Clara frowned. 'I thought Mrs Paradise lived in Oxford, not in St Ives?'

'She moved down to Cornwall a year ago, Mrs Gresham,' Josh said. 'Her husband was killed in a hit and run and she needed a fresh start.'

'Poor woman, how terrible, I am so sorry. It does rather explain things though, doesn't it?'

'In what way?' Josh asked.

'Well, she's suffered a terrible tragedy in her own life and I imagine it has made her particularly sensitive to … how shall I put it, tragedies of the past.'

'Is your husband at home?' Josh asked, knowing he was pushing his luck.

'No he's not, why do you ask, Mr Buchanan, this really is too much?'

'I don't know, I'm sorry, I just wondered.'

'He's playing golf,' Clara said firmly, 'and he won't be back until much later in the day so there is absolutely no point in you waiting to see him.'

Josh recognised the cue and stood up, preparing to leave. 'No, of course not, Mrs Gresham and thank you for your time. It is very reassuring to know that Mrs Paradise was mistaken and that George is safely with his father. I expect you see quite a lot of young George when he is in the country?'

'No, not as much as we would like,' Clara's voice was suddenly unsteady and deeply sad.

'Really?' Josh queried.

'Mr Buchanan, my daughter killed Philip Hope's daughter. It is not the sort of situation that makes for family unity.'

Back in his car Josh drove through the village and at the far end found a lay-by where he stopped, turned off the engine and sat in quiet contemplation for a moment or two. She was a formidable woman, Clara Gresham. Formidable and apparently very sure of herself. Yet all Josh's instincts shouted out that throughout the interview Clara Gresham had been lying through her teeth.

It was after six-thirty and Inspector Penrose was still sitting at his desk. His mound of paperwork seemed to have been breeding during the day. He should not have taken so much time off for lunch with Mrs Paradise. He was in the midst of a murder case, one with no obvious solution on the horizon. Instinctively, though, he felt the lunch had done him good. He felt more able to cope with the horrors that Carly was going through with her treatment. Suddenly he could see the treatment in a more positive light. Maybe, just maybe she would get better, really better. He glanced at his watch, he should be leaving. Supper was always at seven o'clock and Barbara hated him being late. If he left now he could still make it. On cue the telephone rang shrilly and he picked it up expecting it to be Barbara checking up on him.

The voice was instantly recognisable. 'Inspector Penrose?'

'Hello again, Mrs Paradise.'

'I'm sorry to trouble you inspector, twice in one day as it were, but it's just ...' she sounded extremely agitated. '... it's so awful, I can't believe it.'

'What, Mrs Paradise?' he asked patiently, 'what's happened now?'

'The woman, the dead woman you pulled out of the Fal, it's Lizzie Hope.'

Keith's mind did some hurried sorting – Lizzie Hope. 'George Hope's mother?' he asked after a moment.

'Yes,' said Felicity, 'that's right.'

Inspector Penrose let out an audible sigh. 'Are you sure about this, Mrs Paradise?'

'Absolutely sure,' said Felicity, 'at least, as sure as I can be from an artist's impression.'

'So this is absolutely nothing to do with one of your moments of second sight?'

'No,' Felicity replied, 'nothing at all, inspector. I was cleaning some shoes in front of the six o'clock news just now and on Spotlight they were discussing the case and showed the artist's impression of the missing woman which I hadn't seen before because of being in Oxford, I suppose. I recognised her immediately. There is absolutely no doubt about it, it's a very good likeness. What does it mean inspector, maybe George really is in St Ives?' Her voice trailed away, then rallied ... 'those poor parents – first a granddaughter now a daughter.'

'You are absolutely certain of this, Mrs

Paradise?' Inspector Penrose's voice was icy. 'You realise what enormous distress I could cause the Hope family if I start alleging that this is their daughter and it proves not to be the case. You're still very ...' he hesitated, searching for words '... very sensitive about the whole Hope situation. At lunch we more or less agreed that maybe you had imagined that the child in St Ives was George. It could be that your mind playing tricks yet again. There'd be no shame in admitting it.'

Clearly he had said the wrong thing. Felicity's voice was cold in response. 'The news bulletin ended some time ago, Inspector Penrose. I have been sitting here agonising about whether or not to telephone you. I haven't seen the body and only by doing so would I be certain, perhaps not even then,' she hesitated. 'Assuming the artist's impression is a good one though then yes, I am confident your body in the Fal is Lizzie Hope.'

'Right,' said Keith, 'well on that sort of assurance I had better make some enquiries.'

'I can probably help you there,' said Felicity. 'Josh Buchanan, you remember him?'

'Yes, of course,' said Keith, 'he sent me the cuttings on the Hope accident.'

'Exactly, I asked him to check out George's whereabouts for me, so he will have up to date information on the whereabouts of Lizzie Hope's husband and parents. I'll give you his home phone number and mobile.'

'Thank you, Mrs Paradise, that would be most helpful.'

Keith Penrose replaced the receiver thoughtfully. Felicity Paradise was something of an oddball but all his instincts told him he could trust her judgement. His instincts and their previous encounters, left him in no doubt that she was a completely honest, straightforward person. The very last thing she would want to do was inflict any more pain on the Hope family. This was no flight of fancy. For her to have made this call, she had to be very certain indeed as to the identity of the body.

He lifted the telephone again and began dialling his home number. It was going to be a very long night.

Mel found her mother still sitting at the kitchen table when she came home from Annie's.

'Mum, are you alright?'

Felicity shook her head. 'No not really.'

'Why, what's happened?' Mel sat down at the kitchen table and regarded her mother anxiously. 'It's not Jamie or the boys?'

'No, no.' Felicity's troubled eyes regarded Mel. 'This is a bit of a saga Mel, tea of wine?'

'Wine, definitely,' said Mel, 'I'll get it.'

They were into their second glass by the time Felicity had stopped talking.

'It sounds awful,' said Mel, 'but I don't really remember the details of the Hope case. I was in my last year at uni and rather self-centered I suppose. I was aware you weren't having a very good time.'

'Something of an understatement, the press were horrible,' said Felicity, 'they more or less accused me of causing Megan's death.'

'I'm sure you're being over-sensitive there,' Mel said.

Felicity shook her head. 'Dad went crazy, storming round all the newspaper offices, shouting and screaming – it didn't do any good of course.'

Mother and daughter both smiled. 'No it wouldn't have,' said Mel, 'he just upset everybody, right?'

'Absolutely, it made the stories even more viscous if anything.'

'And you are absolutely certain this woman is Lizzie Hope?'

'Oh please,' said Felicity, 'don't you start. Inspector Penrose has been trying to undermine me, too. Of course I can't be absolutely certain but I am as certain as I can be. In which case …' Felicity searched Mel's face as if seeking the answer there, 'in which case, it is not so far fetched to imagine that the little boy I have been seeing in St Ives really is George Hope. With his mother in Truro, it makes much more sense. I've been thinking. The day I saw him and the man he was with both so upset, it would have been the day after the body was discovered. I don't watch much television and I was up in Oxford by the time the local papers came out but I bet there was a lot of media coverage. That day was a very wet one in St Ives so they had probably been watching television. George, or rather the boy who might be George, could have been so upset because he had just learnt that his mother was dead. How truly awful, poor little boy.' Her eyes filled with tears and she fought to control them in front of her daughter.

'Assuming you're right, who was the man with George?'

'I think it must be his grandfather.'

'Maternal or paternal?' Mel asked.

'I think,' Felicity frowned, 'from what I remember, Philip Hope's parents are dead. I think George only has one set of grandparents, his mother's parents, in which case the man with George had just learnt of the death of his daughter.'

It was thirty-six hours before Keith Penrose contacted Felicity again. While she waited for news she found it quite impossible to work and Mel, finding it equally impossible to do anything much to help her mother had continued to spend her days with Annie. It was just after ten on a dull drizzly morning when he finally telephoned with news.

'You were right,' he said, without preamble. 'Clara Gresham identified the body as being that of her daughter, Lizzie, yesterday evening.'

'Oh God,' said Felicity, 'why did she have to do it, poor woman, and not her husband, or her son-in-law, come to that.'

'Philip is abroad and Tom Gresham couldn't cope apparently, delicate constitution. He took to the golf course instead. My wife tells me this is a typical English male reaction by men of a certain age. Strong emotions have to be dealt with in the pub or on the golf course.'

'That may be so but I can't believe he left her to cope with that alone. First her granddaughter now her daughter. She must be in pieces?'

'She's a very formidable woman, apparently,' said Keith. 'She showed impressive control. She said to Jack, my sergeant, afterwards that in many respects her daughter has been lost to her for years because of alcoholism.'

'But the police report, the one I read in the paper,' said Felicity, 'said that there was no drink or drugs found in the body.'

'That's true,' said Inspector Penrose, 'Mrs Gresham told my sergeant that her daughter was trying to give up drink and was obviously meeting with some success.'

'And what about Philip and George, have they been told?' Felicity asked.

'According to Mrs Gresham they are in Germany. She has contacted them and they are already on their way home from Frankfurt. Philip has promised to contact Thames Valley Police as soon as he is home. I think his flight is due in some time today.'

'Are you going to see him, inspector?' Felicity asked.

'I doubt it, not at this stage,' Keith replied. 'He's hardly a suspect. We'll leave it to Thames Valley to interview him and I will see their report.'

'I don't think George is with him,' Felicity said in a small voice, 'I think George is here in St Ives, with his grandfather, which is why Tom Gresham didn't identify his daughter's body.'

'I'd rather gathered that,' said Inspector Penrose, 'but in this particular instance I'm afraid you are uncharacteristically wrong, Mrs Paradise. I am perfectly certain George's grandmother knows where he is and I'm perfectly certain that Thames Valley will be able to confirm shortly that he is with his father. You have been very helpful as always Mrs Paradise and you have done us a great service. As Lizzie Hope was estranged from her family, it could have been months before we had been able to identify the body.'

It was a none too subtle hint to let the matter rest.

Felicity next tried Josh.

'Fizzy, I'm sorry,' he said, 'I've been meaning to

ring you but I've been in a bit of a quandary and busy at work, too.'

'What sort of quandary?' Felicity asked.

'I saw Clara Gresham a couple of days ago, she is …'

'I know who she is, Josh.'

'She told me that George is on a business trip with his father but I got this feeling, Fizzy, I don't know how else to explain it – that she was lying. It's why I haven't rung you. I haven't a shred of evidence, just a feeling she was not being entirely straight with me.'

'So, you haven't heard the developments then?' Felicity asked. 'I thought perhaps Inspector Penrose would have been in touch with you, I gave him your number.'

'No,' Josh said, 'what developments?'

'Inspector Penrose has been involved in a murder case here in Truro. A woman's body was pulled out of the Fal Estuary just over a week ago and they hadn't been able to identify her until now. I saw an artist's impression of her and knew immediately who she was. She was Lizzie Hope, Josh. Clara Gresham identified her daughter's body last night.'

'Dear God,' said Josh, 'how awful, poor woman.'

'Poor Lizzie Hope, come to that,' said Felicity, 'she didn't just fall drunkenly into the Fal, she was strangled first.'

'Does Philip know?' Josh asked.

'Apparently so,' said Felicity. 'The official line is the one you were told. Philip is in Germany on some business trip and took George with him, and in view of the circumstances, they are flying back home today.'

'It's a pity the police couldn't have waited for Philip to identify the body rather than her poor mother. Presumably her husband was with her?'

'No,' said Felicity, 'apparently he couldn't cope, he was playing golf instead.'

Josh let out a whistle. 'That's a very long game of golf,' he said.

'What do you mean?' Felicity asked.

'Tom Gresham was also playing golf when I saw Clara the day before yesterday. He seems a rather shadowy figure.'

Felicity, who was standing out on the balcony watching the comings and goings in the harbour as she spoke to Josh, felt her heart begin to thud at his words. She sat down in order to steady herself.

'He's not a man of mystery, Josh. Don't you see, I've been right all along. It must be him who is with George. That's why I had the feeling that although the boy was unhappy and fearful of something, he was comfortable in his relationship with this older man. I bet it's his grandfather, I bet George Hope is here in St Ives with Tom Gresham.'

'It sounds feasible,' said Josh, mildly, 'but you do

have to ask yourself, why? Why would Clara pretend that the boy is with his father if he was having a holiday in St Ives with his grandfather?'

'I don't know,' Felicity said, somewhat lamely. 'There aren't any photographs of the Greshams, I suppose, in the file?'

'I don't think so,' said Josh, 'no, I'm sure there aren't. All the newspaper coverage at the time was of the immediate family, and of course you …'

'Don't remind me of the newspaper coverage at the time,' Felicity interrupted, 'I still can't bear to be reminded of it.'

'No, sorry,' said Josh.

'If for one moment,' said Felicity, after a pause 'you accept my theory, then one has to ask why grandfather and grandson have gone to ground here with Clara apparently covering up for them and whether there is any connection with the discovery of Lizzie Hope's body only twenty miles away in Truro.'

6

'If for one moment,' said Felicity, 'you accept my theory, then one has to ask why grandfather and grandson have gone to ground here with Clara apparently covering up for them and whether there is any connection with the discovery of Lizzie Hope's body only twenty miles away in Truro.'

This time Felicity's audience was Mel. They were sitting in the kitchen over the remains of supper having talked of nothing but the Hope family all through the meal.

'I was almost jealous of her at the time, you know. All this preoccupation with the Hopes has a sense of déjà vu about it,' Mel said suddenly into the silence that followed Felicity's rhetorical question.

Felicity looked up at her daughter surprised. 'Jealous of who?'

'Megan Hope, of course.'

'Mel, what do you mean?'

'I was in my final year at University when the accident happened, I was really struggling with my law degree and up until then Dad had been very helpful. However when Megan died, the whole focus shifted. Everyone was concentrating on the court hearing, your career and above all poor Megan's death. I remember thinking at the time, Megan Hope had a lot more of my parents' attention in death than I ever had in life.'

Felicity sat back in her chair, genuinely shocked. 'Megan Hope died a horrible death when she was only ten years old Mel. How on earth could anybody be jealous of her? It's a ridiculous and horrible thing to say.'

'Oh, for heaven's sake, of course I'm not really jealous of her and certainly not of what happened to her.' Mel said, defensively. 'I'm just saying I was jealous of the amount of time and thought you gave to her and clearly still do and I wish some of that time and thought had been spent on me. That's all, forget it, it's no big deal. I'll put the kettle on.'

'It is a big deal,' said Felicity, 'if you can feel resentful about the amount of time I've spent thinking about a poor little dead girl, then you must feel very hard done by when it comes to the amount of maternal affection you feel you've enjoyed.'

Mel kept her back to her mother. 'I suppose that's true,' she said, in a small voice, 'but it's never mattered up to now because I've always had Dad.'

'Oh, Mel,' Felicity stood up and went to her daughter, putting her arms around her. Mel remained rigid in Felicity's embrace. 'Mel, loosen up.' Felicity said, leaning her head against Mel's back, 'can't we just talk it all through.'

'That depends on whether you can tear your thoughts away from George Hope for a moment?' Mel retorted, sliding out of her mother's arms and reaching for two mugs. 'Coffee, I presume.'

'Yes please,' said Felicity, feeling both foolish and rejected. She turned away and sat down again. 'Whatever my inadequacies as a mother in the past, Mel,' she began, 'surely it's time to move on. You're twenty-four years old and throughout your childhood you were loved very much by both your mother and your father. It is a tragedy that your father died so young and that he didn't see you marry and have children of your own but he was there for you throughout your childhood and unlike many families, you haven't had to cope with a broken home, step-parents, step-siblings, two different beds to sleep in. I can think of so many little children I've taught over the years who, at the end of a long day at school, are so confused, they have no idea whether they were going home to Mummy or Daddy.'

'There you go again,' said Mel, thumping down the coffee mug in front of Felicity, 'always concerned for other people's children, but never your own.'

'Mel, you are being absolutely ridiculous,' said Felicity, suddenly very angry, 'and childish too.'

'Oh, forget it!' said Mel.

'Mel, just you listen to me for a moment,' said

Felicity, her voice faint with the effort of not losing her temper. 'I have spent the last ten days trying to talk to you, trying to help you work out what you want to do next, trying to find out what really happened in chambers. I desperately want to help you, I'll do anything I can, but you have got to let me in. I can't help very much without at least some degree of cooperation from you.'

'It's amazing how you turn everything round so it's my fault, and you are entirely blameless.'

'Oh, don't be ridiculous, Mel. Come and sit down and let's talk.'

'No thank you,' answered Mel, and stalked out of the kitchen, slamming the door behind her.

Felicity stared down at her cup of coffee, the liquid was still vibrating in the cup, where Mel had banged it on the table. She put her head in her hands, feeling utterly exhausted and very, very alone.

In Truro, Inspector Keith Penrose was also sitting alone in the kitchen. He dare not move. It was the one room in the house where, with the door shut, he could not hear Carly vomiting. Yesterday she had completed the first course of chemotherapy. She should start to feel better now, at least until it began again in a few weeks time, but tonight her reaction was the worst yet. When her hair had started to fall out she had shaved her head and now wore a jaunty surfing beanie which rather suited her.

It was all so terrible, almost unreal. Keith couldn't bear it, couldn't bear what was happening to his little girl. The irony was that she was being so brave, brave and sweet and so anxious not to upset her parents. Keith knew that if this terrible illness had afflicted him, he would have been angry and bitter. He would also have fought it, rallied against it, fighting it every inch of the way. By contrast Carly seemed to be almost complacent in her acceptance of her fate. What did that mean? Could it be that she knew she couldn't influence the outcome? No, he wasn't going to go down that road.

He stood up abruptly. 'Buster!' he called.

Buster, the family's ancient rescue greyhound, lifted one tired eyelid and regarded Keith with a decided lack of enthusiasm.

'Come on, Buster, a walk will do you good. You spend far too much time lounging about in that basket.'

With an audible sigh, Buster lumbered to his feet. There was nothing of the greyhound grace left in Buster, his poor old arthritic joints made his movements awkward and jerky. Keith reached for his coat and Buster's lead and quietly let himself out of the house.

The view from his driveway never ceased to give him pleasure. Keith lived on one of the hills overlooking Truro. From Keith's vantage point, the lights of the city lay below him dominated by the cathedral, towering above the city. Some people were rather rude about Truro Cathedral, claiming it to be a gothic monstrosity. Keith adored it, adored the city and everything about it. He had been born a few miles away at Ladock, the second son of a farmer, and apart from university in Bristol and his police training, he had never left the Duchy and certainly never would now.

He set off down the lane that bordered his garden. With his back to the city lights, the stars were suddenly more dominant in the sky, it really was a beautiful night. With a determined effort to keep his mind from Carly's suffering, he turned his thoughts to the Hope case as he trudged along the lane. There was something about it that was making him feel uneasy. Just because the body had now been identified it had thrown no light whatsoever on the reason for Lizzie Hope's murder, in fact quite the contrary, it had made the case even more baffling. From the police records at the time of Megan's death, Keith had established that Lizzie Hope had already been an alcoholic for some years. After the accident which killed her daughter, it appeared that she continued to drink. Only eighteen months ago her application to have unsupervised access to George had been rejected. The welfare officer allocated to the case had submitted such a damning report to the court concerning Lizzie's continued drinking, her application had not stood a chance.

However, the woman fished out of the Fal had no trace of alcohol in her bloodstream. The pathologist's report had confirmed that the liver was damaged and consistent with that of an alcoholic but at the time she was strangled and dumped in the water, Lizzie Hope had not had a drink for some time.

What could that mean? There was no question of her identity, her mother would hardly have identified the wrong girl, and she had not been long enough in the water to make identification difficult. All Keith's instincts told him he was missing something. Truro like every city had its fair share of crime, particularly in the summer months, but murder was unusual, almost unheard of. Serious assaults tended to be domestic. A woman of thirty-seven, walking around Truro on her own at night, sober and drug free, should have been as safe as houses. So what happened to Lizzie Hope? Discussions with the coastguard had established that the body had probably been dumped at Malpas and brought in on the tide. A search of the shoreline and a house-to-house had produced nothing. Lizzie had never driven a car again, after the death of her daughter so it was logical that she had come to Cornwall by train or plane. They had soon abandoned the possibility of her flying down from the passenger lists at Newquay. So it was the train – and yet no one had seen her, she didn't pick up a taxi at the station – she had materialised apparently out of nowhere, only to die in the Fal.

He reached the stile and looked down at Buster. The old dog turned his back to avoid eye contact and looked longingly towards home.

'Okay, Buster, home time now.'

With a slight wag of his tail, Buster turned with enthusiasm and began walking home with a great deal more energy than he'd displayed thus far.

'You're not a very satisfactory dog to take for a walk,' Keith grumbled. Buster ignored him and plodded on, his mind focused on his basket. Keith glanced at his watch. It was ten-fifteen. Philip Hope should be home by now. He had been due into Heathrow late afternoon and he was to be interviewed by Thames Valley first thing in the morning. Keith wondered how he would be feeling about the death of his wife, the woman who had killed his daughter – relief probably. He tried to imagine himself in a similar situation. The thought of his wife being drunk made him smile. Barbara was so righteous, such a pillar of the establishment, it was an unconceivable notion. Nonetheless, had she got drunk and killed Carly in a car accident, would he have ever forgiven her? Never, never, never.

Keith's unease had still not left him the following morning when he put the phone down after a lengthy conversation with Inspector Andrew Curtis of Thames Valley Police. The transcript of

Inspector Curtis's interview with Philip Hope was on its way. Andrew Curtis considered that everything about Philip Hope had been 'appropriate'. These were Andrew's words not Keith's. The man had been shocked and sad at the news of his former wife's death. However, he had expressed the view that such was the extent of Lizzie's course of self-destruction, it was inevitable that something like this would happen. He appeared to be genuinely shocked that his wife had been strangled before being dumped in the river and he also expressed surprise that she had died without a trace of alcohol in her bloodstream. He confirmed that he had not seen Lizzie for over a year, not since her last abortive attempt to get unsupervised access to George. George had seen his mother twice since then, for an hour or so in the presence of a social worker. However, on the second occasion, Lizzie had turned up drunk and had upset George and since then he had refused to have anything to do with his mother. Philip Hope himself had told Inspector Curtis that he felt it best for both his son and himself to write Lizzie out of their lives, which during the last year they seemed to have been successful in doing. Andrew expressed the view that no one could blame him for that.

'Did you like the man?' Keith asked.

'Not especially,' Andrew said, 'a rather non-descript sort of bloke. Obviously very involved in his business but I would say genuinely fond of his son.'

'Did you meet George?'

'No, no he obviously didn't bring him to the station. I presumed he was still with his grandparents.'

'What do you mean with the grandparents? George was on the business trip with his father.'

'No, no he wasn't. Philip flew into Heathrow alone. The child's been looked after by his maternal grandparents during the last couple of weeks.'

Keith replaced the receiver, stood up and walked over to the door of his office.

'Jack,' he yelled. 'Jack, I want you to go to Bath.' Jack appeared smiling, his boss sounded more positive, more like himself, and a trip to Bath on such a fine day was not an unattractive prospect.

'Now?' he asked mildly.

'Of course now and I'm going to …' he glanced at the file. 'I'm going to Charlbury, near Oxford. If I leave straight away I should be up in Oxford by about eight o'clock. Eight o'clock is the time that a responsible father would have put his young son in bed, bearing in mind that it is a school day tomorrow.'

'Are you going to explain to me what is going on, sir?' Jack asked.

Keith regarded him with amusement. 'That's a little presumptious of you, isn't it, Jack?' They both laughed. 'I've just had a rather strange conversation with Inspector Andrew Curtis of Thames Valley, a very tedious chap, incidentally. He maintains that George never went on the business trip with his father and that he was with his grandmother all the time. The grandmother says that George was with his father, somebody is lying and we need to know where George is.'

'Is it really our business, sir?' Jack asked.

'Of course it's our business, Jack. The boy's mother has been murdered. We need to know exactly where he is and we need to know it now.'

'Sorry sir, yes, of course.'

'Right, so you go and track down the Greshams,' Keith looked at his notes and scribbled down an address for Jack on a piece of paper, 'and I'll go and call on Mr Philip Hope. Let me know as soon as you've made contact.'

'Right sir,' said Jack. It was good to see his boss was once more on the warpath.

A difficult conversation with Barbara followed Keith knew, but much to his relief when he telephoned home, Carly answered.

'Oh, poor you, Dad, you drive carefully now. Will you stay the night up there?'

'Suppose I'll have to,' said Keith, 'I think it is rather a long way to come back tonight.'

'Well, have fun, no talking to any strange women now.'

How did she do it, how did she manage to be so

97

cheerful, he wondered as he walked across the car park. Barbara was at some planning meeting, he discovered, so he would go home, pick up some overnight things and have a cup of tea with Carly. It would be nice to have her to himself, he could spare half an hour before heading to Oxford. He smiled, a sudden thought flashing into his mind. It was Mrs Paradise who normally made the mad, spontaneous trips to Oxford. He knew he was probably wasting his time but there was something nagging at him, some instinct that told him when he got to Oxford he was not going to find George Hope in his bed. In which case, where was he?

The atmosphere at Jericho Cottage the following morning was decidedly frosty, exacerbated by the fact that Mel had more or less finished her painting for Annie.

'There will be some touching up to do after the weekend,' Mel said, 'but Annie's full this weekend so she doesn't want the place to smell of paint.'

In the small cottage the tension between the two women grew. There was no hope of Felicity concentrating on any work and Mel raged around the place like a caged lion.

'Why don't we walk to Zennor and have lunch at the Tinners' Arms and then get a taxi back.'

'Alright,' said Mel. 'If it's not too far for you?'

'Certainly not!' Felicity retorted. 'I've done the

walk several times.'

'It's a bit heavy-going in parts, Mum, a lot of mud and sliding about.'

'I expect I'll manage,' said Felicity, firmly.

The walk did them both good. Clambering over rocks, sliding about in the mud concentrated the mind wonderfully and the scenery was so breathtaking – the sea crawling below them one minute, crashing on the rocks beside them the next as the cliff path took them up and down the cliffs. The colour of the gorse was stunning, the sky, blue. Before long they were stripped down to T-shirts as they trudged along.

'This always reminds me of Scotland,' Felicity said.

Mel nodded. 'Do you remember that holiday we had up on the west coast?' she said.

'Of course,' said Felicity, 'near Oban, that wonderful hotel looking over the sea loch.'

'Loch Melford,' Mel agreed. 'You, I and Jamie trudged for miles and Dad had a very happy holiday, propped up in the bar making wonderful friendships with the locals.'

'It's odd he didn't join us, come to think of it,' said Felicity. 'He used to love walking.'

'He was a bit preoccupied on that holiday,' Mel said, 'he said he had a lot of work to do but he seemed worried about something. Do you remember what it was?'

Felicity shook her head but her mind was racing, trying to calculate what year it had been that they had spent their summer holiday in Scotland. It could well have been the time that Jack Du Plessey, alias Ralph Smithson, had first made contact with Charlie in an attempt to blackmail him. It could well have heralded the beginning of the events that would ultimately lead to Charlie's death. Suddenly, on such a beautiful sunny morning with the majestic scenery all around her, Felicity felt very sick. She stopped walking for a moment and turned away from Mel, looking out to sea. Her heart was hammering in her chest. Most of the time she was able to convince herself that she had come to terms with how and why her husband had died and yet sometimes, like now, she felt that she had still not really addressed the issue, just buried it somewhere where it hurt the least.

'What is it, Mum?' Mel asked, stopping to and peering at her mother.

'Nothing,' Felicity said, hurriedly, 'just feeling sad about your dad.'

'You ought to have a dog,' Mel said after a little silence. 'It would be a companion for you on walks.'

'Not while Orlando's alive, he'd kill it. You know how insanely jealous he is, no puppy would survive more than twenty-four hours!'

They both laughed and the tension eased. By

the time they stopped at the halfway point to share some water and a banana, their relationship was once more on an even keel.

They reached the Tinners', famished, and ordered wine and the homemade steak and kidney pie. They sat by the roaring fire and warmed their aching limbs. It was a delicious experience after the rigours of the walk. Felicity settled back into her chair and let out a huge sigh of contentment. She looked around the bar. There were four other occupied tables and then she saw them, they were just getting up to leave – the boy she thought of as George and the man she imagined to be his grandfather. They seemed contented enough and the man put his hand on the boy's shoulder as he ushered him out of the door. As they went past their table, Felicity lowered her eyes and turned away, she did not want to be spotted by George again. Mel was mercifully in the loo so there was no need to mention the incident to her after last night's outburst. Clearly the Hope family were not a subject for discussion.

By the time they had eaten their way through a delicious lunch and ordered a taxi to take them back to St Ives, it was half-past-three. From the privacy of her bedroom Felicity telephoned Inspector Penrose to be told he was not there and not expected to be back until the morning. She was extremely disappointed, she needed to talk to him, to talk to him now, to offload the feelings churning around in her head.

Sergeant Jack Curnow, like Josh Buchanan before him, had no trouble in finding Juniper Farmhouse on the outskirts of Grittleton. He too was impressed by the gates, the sweeping drive and the imposing old farmhouse. It was mid afternoon and drizzling now, but it could not detract from the charms of the property and its surroundings. He climbed stiffly out of his car. He had been playing rugby at the weekend and had received a very nasty kick in the kidneys which the referee had chosen to ignore. He walked up the door and hammered on the beautifully polished brass doorknob. There was silence. He listened intently and then hammered again. Still silence. Damn, it had been a long way to come to find no one in. He looked around him. There was a battered little Renault Clio parked in the stable yard, that didn't look like it belonged to either of the Greshams and just as the thought was forming in his mind, he heard the distant sound of footsteps on the flag stones, coming towards the front door. The door was opened by a comfortable middle aged woman, a flowery apron stretched across her ample bosom. Her expression was friendly but cautious.

'What can I do for you?' she asked.

'I'm looking for the Greshams, are they in?'

'No they're not. They're away.'

'Oh,' said Jack. 'Could you tell me where?'

'No I certainly couldn't, it's no business of yours, now be off with you.'

With studied calm, Jack produced his warrant card. 'I'm really sorry to trouble you,' he said, turning on his most charming smile, 'but we really do need to contact them urgently.'

'Why?' There was alarm in the comfortable face.

'It's a personal matter, I can't discuss it. They won't have gone away without leaving a forwarding address. I presume you're the housekeeper.'

'No I'm not and yes, they have gone without giving me a forwarding address.'

'That's a little odd, isn't it?' Jack said.

'No, not especially,' was the defensive reply.

'Could you tell me your name please?'

'What's it got to do with you?'

'I need to know the name of anyone who is failing to help the police with their enquiries,' he said, evenly.

The face flushed bright scarlet. 'My name is Mary Jenkins,' she said. 'I live nearby and I work for the Greshams doing a bit of cleaning and ironing three times a week, normally. I'm not a housekeeper, I'm just a help. I don't know their business and they don't know mine. They told me they were away for a few days. It's no problem to me, I have a key, in fact I get on better when they're not around.'

'Did they say when they would be back?' Jack asked.

'No, they just said they would be away for a few days.'

'I still think it is odd they didn't leave you a telephone number – supposing something went wrong with the house.'

'What's to go wrong with the house?' said Mary, 'I'm here to look after it.'

'What about a mobile?' Jack said, suddenly inspired.

'They don't hold with mobiles, and nor the more do I,' said Mary, firmly.

'Do you know their grandson, George?' Jack asked.

'Of course I know George, I've known him since he was a baby, a dear little lad.'

'Is he with them then?' Jack asked.

'How should I know?'

'Well, Mary Jenkins,' said Jack, 'thank you very much indeed for all your help,' and with that he strode back to the car.

Jack drove too fast down the drive and out onto the lane. The farm was in a hollow and he drove up the lane to a layby formed by the entrance to a field. Here he stopped and got out of the car, taking lungfuls of fresh air. The rain had stopped now but it was still dull and overcast. He was angry with himself. The boss would have been charming with the wretched old biddy and extracted far more information from her. He must learn to curb his impatience. They had taken one look at each other, he and Mary Jenkins, and instantly disliked each other and the interview was doomed from the start. Hands in his pockets, he wandered through the opening into the field and gazed out across the countryside. From his vantage point, he could see Juniper Farmhouse below him and he realised that although when in the valley, the house appeared to be completely isolated, in fact there was another farm very close to it, tucked into another hollow just the far side of where the Juniper Farmhouse barns appeared to end. How could he get to that farm he wondered – there certainly wasn't access from this lane. On a hunch he climbed back into the car, drove further up the lane and sure enough there was a left hand turning. He took it and within a few minutes found himself driving into a very different property from its next door neighbour.

This was a true working farm. A half-dead tractor appeared to be abandoned just off the driveway, a rusty old plough a few yards further on. Why was it that farmers were so notoriously bad at looking after their machinery, Jack wondered? He pulled into a muddy yard and climbed gingerly out of the car. A collie dog was lying by a stable door, nose on paws. It raised its head and eyed him suspiciously but made no attempt to affect a greeting.

'Anyone about?' Jack asked it. The dog ignored him. 'Hello,' Jack shouted hopefully, 'is anyone around?'

The stable door opened and an elderly figure shambled out. He was dressed in ancient overalls with a piece of baler twine tied around his waist which seemed to be holding the whole garment together. His flat cap was pulled well down over his eyes so it was difficult to see his expression.

'What do you want?' he asked.

'I'm really sorry to trouble you,' said Jack, 'but I'm looking for Mr and Mrs Gresham.'

'Well you've come to the wrong farm here,' grumbled the old man. 'They're over the hill there, Juniper Farmhouse. If you go back along the ...'

'Yes, I know that,' said Jack, 'I've been there, spoken to their housekeeper, but they're away.'

There was a cackle. 'So what do you think I'm going to do then, magic them back for you?' When the old man laughed, his appearance was even more startling. One of his teeth seemed to have worked loose from the gums and waggled slightly with the vibration of mirth. Jack tried to look away but the sight was riveting.

'No, no, of course not,' he said, with a forced smile. 'I'm just trying to locate them and I thought you might have an idea where they've gone.'

'What's it to you anyway?' the old man asked.

'I'm a policeman,' said Jack and produced his warrant card.

'They're not in any trouble, are they?' the old man asked.

'No, I'm just making some enquiries. Actually I'm trying to locate their grandson, you wouldn't know where he was, would you?'

'Nice little boy that George,' said the old man, 'he comes up and helps me sometimes, loves the farm, he's got a way with animals. You can tell it in children from the earliest age. Some who come up here are only interested in the machinery and others take to the animals right away. George is one of those, he helped me deliver a lamb in the Spring, didn't upset him at all. It was a difficult birth and he was a great help. He's alright, is he?'

'As far as we know,' said Jack, 'I'm just trying to find him.'

'Why?'

Jack hesitated there seemed no point in keeping anything from this old man. 'His mother died a week ago.'

'That Lizzie, drunk I suppose, was she? What did she do, kill herself in a car crash this time?'

'No, no, she was ...' Jack hesitated, 'she was murdered.'

'Well I be,' said the old boy, 'there's a thing. That poor little boy, what a lot he's been through, no wonder you want to find him.'

'So can you help at all?' Jack asked.

'I would but I can't, they don't tell me anything. Bit stuck up for me, they are. I don't think they really like George coming up here very much. Reckon I'll teach him some bad habits, probably might, too.' Again the terrible cackle and the waggling tooth.

'I'm sorry,' said Jack, 'can I ask your name?'

'Suppose so, my name's Norman, Norman Jenkins.'

'Ah,' said Jack, 'are you anything to do with Mary down at Juniper Farmhouse?'

'Yes, that's my wife.'

'Well you might have said so,' said Jack, exasperated.

'You didn't ask!' another laugh, another waggle.

'So where do the Greshams normally go on holiday?' Jack persisted.

'Cornwall usually, St Ives. They used to have a cottage down there, but they sold it in order to buy that Lizzie a flat in Oxford after the accident – spoilt rotten that one, even after killing her little girl.' Bingo, thought Jack, so Mrs Paradise may have been right all along. 'Thanks Mr Jenkins,' he said, 'you've been really helpful.'

'Nice to know I've helped the Constabulary,' the old man said, sarcastically and Jack left him cackling away, tooth waggling madly and headed back towards Grittleton.

7

Keith made good time to Oxford. As he dropped down onto the ring road, he looked a little wistfully at the dreaming spires ahead of him then resolutely turned left and headed out towards Woodstock and ultimately Charlbury. He arrived in the little town of Charlbury and found the Hope's house easily enough. It was with deep satisfaction that he saw there were lights on behind the already drawn curtains. He circled the town and spied the Bell Inn. By half past eight he had showered, changed his shirt and had a much needed cup of coffee.

As he walked up the street towards the Hope's house, he reflected on his telephone call from his sergeant a couple of hours earlier. Although Jack's trip to Bath had been largely abortive, it had proved interesting and helpful for his forthcoming interview with Philip Hope. Like Jack he thought it was inconceivable that a couple should leave their valuable home and not give anyone an indication of their forwarding address and telephoné number, and, of course, there was the really startling piece of information was that the family often holidayed in St Ives. The thought that Mrs Paradise had been right all along bought a smile of amusement – he should have learnt by now, she had an uncanny habit of being right. Whatever it was with her – this intuition, second sight, natural instinct, call it what you like – it rarely let her down. When she told him the child she had seen in distress in St Ives was George Hope, he should have believed her.

Mulberry House was an attractive property and to his untutored eye it looked like a Georgian town house with a freshly painted blue door. He knocked gently, trying not to make too much noise with a child in the house. The man who answered the door, almost immediately, perfectly fitted the description given to him by his Thames Valley colleague. He was in fact entirely non-descript of appearance. His hair was thinning, a mousy colour, he was medium height with the slightly unhealthy looking skin tone of someone who spent too much time indoors. He had reasonably put together features, though not memorable – indeed, the only memorable thing about Philip Hope was his eyes, a piercing light blue, slightly hooded, and although his tone was friendly.

'Good evening, how can I help you?'– the blue eyes were hostile and suspicious.

'I'm sorry to trouble you, sir, and particularly at this time of night,' Keith began, 'but I am a police officer.'

'Nothing more wrong, I hope,' Philip said. 'I've had enough shocks for one week.'

'No sir, I wondered whether I just might come and talk to you for a few minutes. It concerns your wife's death. My name is Inspector Keith Penrose. I'm in charge of your wife's case.'

'Ex-wife, inspector, and surely you could have come during the day rather than this late in the evening?'

Keith continued to eat humble pie. 'I really am sorry, sir, but I have just driven up from Cornwall.'

The blue eyes registered a hint of alarm. 'Then you'd better come in.' Philip led the way into a rather cheerless drawing room. The room was beautifully proportioned, with a lovely old marble fireplace in which sat a rather drab bunch of dried flowers.

'Would you like a drink? Sorry, I didn't catch your name.'

'Detective Inspector Keith Penrose. Well, I haven't got to walk very far this evening, a small scotch would be most welcome, sir.'

'Sorry inspector, I didn't mean an alcoholic drink, we don't have alcohol in this house. Tea or coffee?'

Keith felt wrong-footed and awkward, not a situation he enjoyed. Already he didn't like this man. 'Coffee would be fine, sir, thank you. White no sugar.'

'If you'd like to wait here then, inspector, I

won't be a moment.'

Left to his own devices Keith studied the room. Like the man, it had no distinguishing features except on the mantelpiece where there stood a picture a small boy – flaxen haired, the same blue eyes as his father but laughing and friendly. He was posing by what looked like, a brand new bike. The door opened and Philip entered carrying two mugs of coffee on a tray.

'Is this your son, George, sir?' Keith asked.

Philip nodded.

'Is he with you at the moment?'

'No,' Philip answered, shortly. 'He is staying with his grandparents near Bath.'

For the moment Keith decided to let it rest. He noted his heart was beating a little faster, a sure sign that his instincts were telling him there was something wrong. Philip indicated a chair. 'Do sit down, inspector. What is it I can do for you? I really can't be very long. I've got a mountain of work to catch up on, I've just come back from Frankfurt.'

'I'm aware of that, sir and I'll make this as speedy as I can. As I explained, I am in charge of the investigation into your ex,' he put emphasis on the word, 'ex-wife's death and I need as much background as possible. I felt it would be helpful to talk to you direct rather than just read a report. That's why I am here.'

Philip looked irritated and slightly edgy, Keith

thought. He sat back in his chair, crossed his leg one way and then crossed it the other way. This was not a relaxed man.

'I really have nothing to add,' he said. 'I gave a full statement to your colleague from Thames Valley Police, presumably you read it?'

'Not yet,' said Keith.

'Then I suggest you do so and had you done so, I imagine you could probably have saved us both a lot of time.'

'I read the file,' Keith said, 'and I am well able to understand that you felt a great deal of animosity towards your ex-wife.'

'If you're suggesting I killed her, I wasn't even in the country.'

'No,' said Keith, genuinely surprised by the reaction. 'No, I wasn't suggesting that. What I am trying to say is that I appreciate you probably view her death as an accident waiting to happen. With her record of drinking, it was only a matter of time before she did herself some serious harm.'

Philip looked surprised and watching carefully, Keith saw him relax a little.

'You're right, inspector, very perceptive of you. When your colleague told me what had happened, I was shocked, naturally, and sad – she is, was, after all my son's mother, but I can't say I was surprised.'

'Not even about her being strangled?

'Yes,' Philip said, 'yes, that was a surprise. Are

you sure you're right about how she died, inspector?'

'Oh, yes, sir, quite right,' Keith assured him.

'Well, I suppose she rubbed someone up the wrong way. She could be very abusive and rude when she was drunk,' Philip sounded horribly complacent.

'But that's just it, sir, she wasn't drunk, I presumed you were told that.'

'Then it must have been a very temporary abstinence. She has been drinking steadily for the last fifteen years.'

'There was absolutely no trace of alcohol in her body, sir, although, there was evidence of liver damage. The pathologist is of the view that she hadn't drunk for some time. There was only mild cirrhosis and evidence was that the liver was starting to rejuvenate itself.'

'What are you saying exactly?' said Philip.

'I'm not sure what I am saying,' Keith admitted. 'I suppose I'm suggesting that the drunken accident you envisaged happening to your wife because of her addiction doesn't seem to fit the description of how she died. She died violently, yes, but not as a result of drink. I was wondering whether you have any ideas, any theories of your own?'

Philip shook his head. 'I hear what you say and what the pathologist says, but I would imagine that her death is somehow linked to her drinking.'

'And what do you think she was she doing in Truro?'

'Inspector, I have really no idea. For the last five years, my ex-wife's whereabouts have not been of concern to me.'

'Since your daughter's death?' Keith interjected.

'Yes,' said Philip, 'since my daughter's death, I have had nothing to do with my ex-wife. I have no idea what she did or where she was on a day-to-day basis. We met across a court room a couple of times and George has seen her once or twice a year. I don't even know where she was living recently. The only address we have ever been given for her was her parents home but she goes there rarely, I understand.'

'Do you get on well with your in-laws?' Keith asked.

'Yes, indeed,' said Philip. 'George is very fond of them. My parents are dead, so they are the only grandparents he has and they have been a constant in his life.'

'And you say he is with them now?'

'Yes, that's right,' said Philip.

'Would it surprise you to know that they've told us that George was with you on your business trip?'

'I'm afraid you must be mistaken.'

'I can assure you I am not,' said Keith, 'and that is really why I'm here. They say George is with you, you say George is with them. The question I am asking myself, Mr Hope, is – where is George?'

'He's with his grandparents.' Philip Hope was

becoming agitated now. 'It's quite possible they may have decided to take him on a little trip, they do sometimes.'

'And not tell you? Sir, that seems rather strange.'

'They know I have complete faith in them and their care of George, they also know I am extremely busy at the moment. Furthermore, inspector, I don't think this is any of your damn business.'

'There sir, I'm afraid you're wrong,' said Keith. He could feel himself bristling with anger, he must control himself, he really did not like this man. 'I'm trying to put myself in your shoes, sir. Presumably George has been told that his mother has died?'

'Yes,' said Philip, 'yes, he has.'

'And who told him?'

'His grandparents.'

'Have you seen him since?'

'No,' said Philip, 'I've only just got back from my business trip, you know that.'

'It all seems a bit odd to me, sir. I'm a father, too. Whatever the relationship the boy may have had with his mother, however estranged from her he might be, I would have felt, in your shoes, I needed to be with my son at such a delicate time. He must have a lot of questions, he's not a baby anymore. He also must have loved his mother once.'

'She was never a mother to him,' Philip Hope burst out. 'It's a wonder Megan and George survived

116

as long as they did in her care. She was a terrible mother – forgetting to feed them, forgetting to pick them up from school – George knows he is far better off without her.'

'I wonder if that's true, sir. My experience of children, even severely abused children, is that they display a commendable loyalty to their birth parents. It's a tragedy really – however inadequate one is as a parent, while they are small at least, children have this uncanny habit of going on caring.' Just for a moment his thoughts strayed to Carly, he forced them back into line.

Philip Hope must have seen the strength of his emotion. 'That sounded rather heartfelt, inspector.'

'I see a great many sad children in my profession,' Keith replied, evenly. 'Tell me, sir, is it possible that George's grandparents may have taken him on holiday to St Ives?'

'Possible, I suppose,' Philip Hope said, defensive again.

'Have you been to St Ives?'

'Yes, indeed. Not for a year or two, but certainly it is a place we've been on holiday.'

'And the Gresham's, have they holidayed there often?'

'Yes, in fact they introduced me to the town. They used to have their family holidays there when Lizzie was a little girl. They owned a cottage there until a few years ago.'

'What if I told you that George had been seen in St Ives the week his mother died. Would that surprise you?'

Philip frowned. 'Seen by whom?'

'That is a confidential matter. Can you just answer the question, sir?'

'Yes, well I suppose it would surprise me. I thought he was at home with his grandparents.'

'It seems to me, sir, that you are not at all sure where your son is at the moment.'

'Oh for God's sake,' said Philip. 'I have told you and told you, he is with his grandparents.'

'I accept that,' said Keith, 'but what I would like to know is where are his grandparents? It appears, sir, that you are quite unable to answer the question.'

Twenty minutes later Keith was nursing a scotch at the bar of the Bell Inn. He had parted on very bad terms with Philip Hope having insisted on taking a photograph of his son.

'As far as I am concerned sir, until I can find Mr and Mrs Gresham and your son, I am treating the boy as missing person.'

He took the photograph that he had been given so reluctantly out of his wallet and studied it for a moment. It had been taken during the summer, Philip said. George was sitting on a bean bag in the garden. He was less carefree and smiling than he had been in the photograph with his bike – in fact he

118

looked positively forlorn. Hardly surprising, poor little chap, having that bloke for a father.

The bar had more or less cleared and the young man behind the bar was polishing glasses. 'Do you know Philip Hope?' Keith asked. 'Mulberry House, just up the road.'

'I know who you mean,' the barman said. 'He doesn't come in here, he's not a drinking man, but I see him around. He's got a young son, hasn't he?'

'That's him. Do you know anything about him?'

The barman shrugged. 'I heard that there was a tragedy,' he frowned trying to recall what he had heard. 'He had a daughter, she was killed in a car accident. Am I right?'

'Yes,' said Keith, 'that's right. It's just the man and his boy now.'

'As I say, we don't see them in here, not really. I know him well enough to say good morning if we pass in the street. Nice child though, very friendly, amazing hair almost white. May I ask why you're enquiring about him?'

'I'm doing business with him. He seems a straight enough kind of guy but I'm always wary about doing business with people I don't know.'

'He's not short of a bob or two, I can tell you that – lovely house plus a very smart BMW. The boy is at a private school in Oxford somewhere. Depends whose buying and whose selling but if you're selling then I should think you'll get your bills paid.'

'Thanks,' said Keith, 'in which case I think I'll have the other half of that scotch.'

Keith telephoned Felicity from a lay-by as he joined the A30 the following morning.

'I'm glad you rang,' she said, 'I've been trying to get hold of you. Are you back in Truro?'

'No, not quite, another hour and half I would imagine. I was hoping you could come into the station, there's something I need to show you.'

'I've got some news for you too,' said Felicity. He glanced at the clock on the dashboard.

'Could you make it by eleven-thirty?'

'I'll be there,' she said.

Keith looked very tired and strained, Felicity thought when she entered the office. 'How is your daughter, inspector?'

He shook his head wearily. 'Not very good at the moment, the treatment, you know ...' His voice trailed away.

'I'm sorry,' Felicity could think of nothing else to say, and he must have sensed her awkwardness, for he rallied and offered the attempt of a smile.

'Now, what have you got to tell me?' he asked.

'I've seen them again.'

'What, your mysterious man and boy?' Keith asked.

'Yes, at Zennor this time, at the Tinners' Arms.

My daughter and I walked over from St Ives for lunch and there they were. They didn't see me, I made sure they didn't, I didn't want to frighten the little boy again.'

Keith felt in the breast pocket of his jacket and pulled out his wallet. He carefully extracted the photograph and handed it to Felicity. 'Does the child look anything like this?'

Felicity stared at the photograph, closed her eyes for a moment and when she opened the again, Keith saw she was close to tears.

'Yes,' she said, 'yes, that's him. Where did you get this photograph?'

'I extracted it with some difficulty from Philip Hope last night. It is a photograph of his son.'

'Then, I haven't been imagining things, that child really is George Hope.

8

'I don't suppose they can launch a proper manhunt?' Annie said.

Felicity and Annie were sitting in the kitchen of Cormorant Cottage. 'Why not?' Felicity asked.

'Well, he's not really missing, is he? Your inspector says that the father is happy that he's with the grandparents and the grandparents have just gone away for a few days, probably to St Ives or Zennnor. There's no law against that.'

'Something's definitely not right,' said Felicity, 'and Inspector Penrose feels the same. Imagine, Annie, the poor little boy has just lost his mother. It doesn't matter what the circumstances – can you imagine being his father and not wanting to be with him?'

'No, I can't,' said Annie, 'but then it's a funny old world these days, families are different to how they used to be. Maybe George is closest to his grandparents and the father thinks it's better that he is with them at the moment. After all the Greshams are his mother's parents. Maybe he is particularly close to his grandmother, maybe she is a substitute mother, maybe the father thinks she is the best person to comfort him.'

'All of that is entirely logical, I agree,' said Felicity, 'and I would find it much easier to accept that I was fussing unnecessarily if it wasn't for the fact that Inspector Penrose feels the same as I do.'

'Does he' Annie asked, 'has he told you so?'

'Well, not exactly,' said Felicity. 'Clearly he didn't like Philip Hope and clearly he thought that his duty as a father was not to be messing about with his business but comforting his son on the loss of his mother. He also thinks it's odd that, apparently, Philip doesn't know where the boy is, just that he is with his grandparents – well somewhere.'

'Well that doesn't make any sense I agree. That father should be telephoning the boy every night, saying goodnight to him, seeing how his day was, that sort of thing.'

'Exactly,' said Felicity. 'The whole relationship seems pretty unnatural and when you consider that he is a single parent and has been for some years in reality, you'd expect there to be, if anything, a closer bond.'

'My Billy is on holiday at the moment,' Annie said, 'he's thirty-three and lives in Australia but I know where he is.'

Felicity smiled at her, leant across and patted her arm. Billy was Annie's youngest son. She couldn't bear the fact that he lived and worked in Australia and she hadn't seen him now for over two years. Felicity had done her best to help since she had come into Annie's life. She had tried to persuade her to e-mail her son and had spent hours with Annie sitting at her own laptop, but it was not a medium with which Annie felt comfortable. Equally she had a great distrust of telephoning abroad and although Felicity had found special numbers to dial for cheap calls to Australia, Annie wouldn't use them. She wrote to her boy every day and to his great credit, Billy wrote back at least once a week.

'Not every parent is as good as you are, Annie,' she said.

'If I was so good a parent what is he doing the other side of the world?'

They had travelled this path before, many times. 'Because you gave him the confidence to go for what he wanted in life and what he wants in life at the moment is to work in Australia.'

'How's your girl?' Annie said, obviously anxious to change the conversation.

'Not good,' said Felicity, 'at least not good with me. How has she been with you?'

Annie smiled. 'Hardworking.'

'Well, she wouldn't dare be anything else, you're a hard taskmaster, Annie.'

Annie put her head on one side and regarded Felicity quizzically for a moment. Whenever she did this Felicity always felt uncomfortable under the scrutiny of so much shrewdness.

'She doesn't want to talk about anything at the moment,' Annie said, 'but she is carrying a burden of some sort, something she is not prepared to talk about.'

Felicity frowned. 'Do you think so, are you saying you think something is really wrong?'

'I don't know what you mean by really wrong but, dear of her, she's carrying something – to do with her work I think.'

'She is very resentful towards me,' Felicity said in a small voice. 'She even accused me of caring more about the Hopes than about her the other night, and she is very jealous of her brother.'

'I think she still has some growing up to do,' said Annie.

'She's nearly twenty-four,' said Felicity.

'Nonetheless, she has spent all her life struggling to pass these exams, working so hard, so single mindedly. I think that while she is obviously very clever at what she does, she has neglected the emotional side of her life. She says she hasn't had a boyfriend for years, beautiful girl like that, it makes no sense, my girl, does it?'

'No it doesn't,' Felicity agreed. 'I feel badly about it all now. I feel I should have tried to take the pressure off her but she was so focused and of course her father encouraged her. She certainly wants to be as good as he was and sees him as some sort of role model, an idol almost. Looking back on it,' Felicity said, thoughtfully, 'I think he probably encouraged her. One can't help enjoying a little hero worship and Charlie was very much flesh and blood like the rest of us. What do you think I should do, Annie?'

'Bide your time,' said Annie, 'do as I said, be gentle, keep off the subject of anything controversial, make time for her, feed her well and wait. She will tell you what it is that is upsetting her when she's good and ready.'

'In the meantime, though, I seem to be upsetting her by worrying about George Hope. I just can't get him out of my mind, Annie, I feel so responsible for him.'

'You can't feel like that, my girl. You can't take on the problems of the world.'

'George Hope isn't the problems of the world. If I had just tried a bit harder, been a bit quicker, he would still have his sister.'

'Don't go down that road,' Annie said firmly.

Felicity gave her a sad little smile. 'I'll go down that road, Annie, for the rest of my life.'

Martin Tregonning guided his battered old Land Rover down the hill to St Ives. It was a beautiful sunny morning and being so early on a Sunday morning, there was practically no one about except for the odd dog walker. St Ives hadn't changed, of course, but he had, he knew, and he was ready now to come home. He parked his car on a loading bay on the Wharf and crossed the road to the harbour. The tide was out and he clambered down steps onto the sand and gave a great sigh of contentment. That wonderful quality of light that only seemed to exist in St Ives, struck him afresh as it always did when he had been away. The brightness of the blue sky, the yellow of the sand – it was more like a child's painting than reality. He walked across the sand towards the sea, hands in his pockets, looking about him with pleasure. Why he had decided St Ives was home he could not think. His family had farmed for generations on the Lizard and until he was twelve, he had never even set foot in St Ives but now, it was where he felt he was ready to put down roots. The family farm was sold, his parents now lived in a bungalow in Helston and his wife had been dead for well over a year. In many respects it seemed longer, as if he had been struggling on alone all his life. It had taken him so many years to find Helen and then to lose her again so quickly, and the baby.

He had spent the last few months travelling across Europe, telling himself that he was taking the time out to finish the book he was writing. In reality, he was just running away. It was only in the last few weeks that he had managed to turn and face his grief. For a few weeks he had rented what was little more than a goat hut almost on the beach on the Greek island of Kos; there alone and undisturbed he had howled out his grief night after night – it was a purging. Helen would always be a part of him, an ache that would never go away, but there were treasured memories, too, and he would hold them close to him for, generous and sweet as she had been, he knew that Helen would like to be remembered with happiness not sadness. He reached the water's edge and turned and faced the town. It looked wonderful. The seagulls swooped and cried, there were one or two people walking along the Wharf now carrying Sunday papers. Two little boys were already busy building a giant of a sandcastle. To his right a couple of horses were being ridden along the water's edge, their nostrils flared with excitement as they danced in and out of the waves. In the distance he could see a group of people gathered around the Harbour Office. There would be friends among them for Martin had been a volunteer coastguard, and would be again. With probate settled at last he had just enough money to buy a little cottage but in the meantime, while he searched, he knew where he was going. Whistling, he began striding off across the sand towards the town and Cormorant Cottage.

'You shouldn't give an old woman shocks like this,' she scolded, after shrieking and throwing her arms around him and then dragging him into her kitchen while she began cooking him a breakfast.

'I'm sorry, Annie,' said Martin, 'I should have telephoned you first. I was hoping you had a spare room for a few weeks while I do some house hunting.'

Annie was expertly flipping bacon on the grill. She stopped, a huge smile spreading across her funny little face. 'House-hunting, does that mean you're coming back to us, my bird, and staying here?'

His handsome face broke into a smile to match her own. 'I had to come back to my favourite girl, didn't I?' he said.

'If only I was thirty years younger,' said Annie. 'Have you seen Felicity yet?'

Martin shook his head. 'No I thought I ought to organise a room with you first. I didn't want her to feel she would have to offer to put me up.'

'She couldn't anyway, she's full,' said Annie.

'Whose staying?'

'Wait and see,' said Annie, grinning.

An hour later Martin was unpacked and showered, and presented himself at Jericho Cottage. He was looking forward enormously to seeing Felicity again. They had shared so much together, heavens, had nearly died together. Above even that, though, they had a common link, an inseparable bond – they had both lost their life partner and were still struggling to cope with the fact. He rapped on the door full of anticipation at seeing his old friend.

The door opened and he stared in utter amazement. There, framed in the doorway, was one of the most beautiful young women he had ever seen – long blonde hair, huge blue eyes and something very familiar about the shape of her face.

'I'm sorry,' he stammered, 'I was looking for Felicity Paradise.'

'Well you've found her, 'I'm Mel, her daughter.'

'Of course you are,' Martin smiled, 'you couldn't possibly be anyone else. You're the terrifyingly high powered lawyer, the apple of your mother's eye.'

'You know about me?' Mel said. 'Then you have the advantage of me, who are you?'

'My name is Martin Tregonning.'

'Martin Tregonning,' Mel pointed a finger at him and smiled. 'Then I know all about you, too. You were the hero of the hour. You and Mum routed the evil bastard who – what was his name?'

'Ralph Smithson,' said Martin.

'That's it, Ralph Smithson who was drug smuggling and all sorts and who, incidentally,' her face hardened, her smile left it, 'and who,' she said faltering, 'was responsible for the death of my dad.'

'He won't be troubling anyone again,' Martin said, feeling a rush of sympathy for this beautiful girl, clearly still mourning the loss of her father. 'I am pleased to tell you that South African jails are not nearly as pleasant as ours and I am confident that he is there for the duration.'

They stood on the doorstep smiling at one another. He really was incredibly good looking, Mel thought. She tried to judge his age, it was hard to tell, forty maybe. Her mother was a dark horse. She had talked a lot about Martin Tregonning but never once mentioned what a babe he was.

'Come in, come in,' she said awkwardly. 'We've got a joint in the oven for Sunday lunch. You will stay won't you – it's a bit bleak trying to make an occasion on Sunday when it's just Mum and me? Go upstairs, she is out on the terrace, I'll fetch a bottle of wine.' Mel smiled as she heard her mother's shrieks of delight as she uncorked a bottle and fetched three glasses, feeling absurdly grateful for Martin Tregonning's presence. Things were still very strained between her and her mother. She knew she had behaved like an ass. Her mother was a good woman and had done her best. The fact that she felt in such turmoil was not her mother's fault. That was the trouble with motherhood, Mel thought, mothers were always expected to put things right and what was wrong with her now, her mother just couldn't fix. She was still smiling a little ruefully as she walked out onto the terrace.

The three of them spent a lovely day together. It was warm enough to eat lunch on the terrace. They drank too much wine, then walked on the beach and were now lounging about in the kitchen with the Sunday papers. Orlando had climbed straight onto Martin's lap, Mel noted, which was a rare honour. She said as much. Martin grinned at her with his attractive lop sided smile. 'Don't think for one moment I don't realise how privileged I am,' he said, 'for some reason Orlando and I have an unshakable bond. I think it might be because we are both incredibly lazy.'

'Nonsense,' said Felicity. 'You're just brilliant with animals. It's being raised on a farm I expect. Tell me, how is your book going?'

'Don't ask,' Martin said. 'Shall we just say I've been a bit 'Orlando-like' about it. I think I've managed about half a chapter since I saw you last.'

'What's the book about?' Mel asked.

'Tropical gardens, probably not your thing.'

'Martin is a tree man really,' said Felicity, 'only there aren't too many trees in West Cornwall so he's become sidetracked into tropical gardens instead. So what happens next,' Felicity asked, 'once the book's finished?'

'I don't know yet. Buying a cottage, is the first priority.' He hesitated. 'The new owner of Boswithey is apparently interested in offering me my old job back but I couldn't do that, I couldn't go back.' His face clouded for a moment.

'Going back is never a good idea,' Felicity said, gently, 'you need a fresh start, a new challenge.'

'Don't I know it,' said Martin. 'I'd really like to do something on my own, start my own business, I

132

just can't think what.'

'Don't rush it,' said Felicity, 'you're looking so much better, so much happier – you've come a long way, Martin.'

Martin glanced at Mel who appeared engrossed in the *Telegraph*. 'And you?' he asked gently.

Felicity smiled. 'I'm getting there.' She stood up, stifling a yawn. 'After all that wine and walking, I'm going to have a siesta. A cup of tea in one hour please, if you two are still around.'

'I'd better be going too,' Martin said after Felicity had left, making absolutely no attempt to move.

'I'll put the kettle on,' said Mel. 'Have a cup of tea before you go.'

'Is your mother really getting better?' he asked.

'I think so,' said Mel. 'It's hard to imagine what it must be like to lose your husband.'

'No,' said Martin his face taking on a shuttered look.

'Sorry, that wasn't very tactful of me,' said Mel, mortified.

Martin was quick to reassure. 'No problem, I'm trying to develop a thick skin, that's my plan. So please continue to be as tactless as possible. It would be a great help, good training.'

They smiled at one another. 'Actually,' said Mel, 'Mother is involved in another case. I notice she didn't mention it to you over lunch which is surprising really, she's absolutely obsessed.'

'Really,' said Martin, 'on the track of another criminal?'

'No, no, more complex than that. If you've got the time, I'll tell you, I know she wouldn't mind.'

By the time Mel had finished the story of the Hope case Martin's face was creased with concern, his blue eyes full of compassion.

'God, how awful for her, I had no idea she had been through that as well as losing her husband.'

'Everyone thinks she's imagining George,' Mel said.

'What you mean he's one of her flights of second sight?'

'No, no, nothing like that,' said Mel, 'not one of her funny moments, just that she has transferred all her guilt and feelings of inadequacy into trying to save today's George, having failed to help him when he was a baby.'

'That doesn't sound like your mother to me,' said Martin.

'I have to admit it doesn't to me either,' Mel said, 'anyway it looks like your buddy, Inspector Penrose, is starting to believe her at last.'

Josh was into his second glass of burgundy, propping up the bar at the Wig and Pen Club in Fleet Street. It was ridiculous to be drinking so fast and furiously at lunch time, it didn't suit him any more, but he was nervous. No not nervous he told himself, just apprehensive. Out of the blue he had received a telephone call from Michael Ferguson suggesting lunch. There was no logical reason for them to meet, certainly not socially. Josh had known Michael most of his life since he was a fat toddler, kid brother of Josh's boyhood friend, but they had never been close, the age gap was too great. He sensed that the meeting had to be something to do with Mel.

Josh had almost finished his second glass of wine when Michael Ferguson walked into the bar, raising an arm in greeting to several diners as he threaded his way through the tables. He was already something of a flamboyant figure, a typical barrister destined for great things, Josh thought a little enviously. He was tall – it was always good to be tall if you were a barrister – several inches taller than Josh himself, with dark hair and a haughty aristocratic face, high cheek bones and clever calculating eyes. It was not a particularly nice face but an arresting one.

'Josh, hello,' Michael said, shaking Josh's hand. 'I'm so sorry I'm late. The judge saw the way to end a very tedious case and was so excited by the prospect he pressed on into the lunch break in order to put it out of it's misery. What are you drinking?'

'A glass of house burgundy,' Josh said.

'A glass of burgundy and a tonic water,' Michael

called to the barman.

Oh this tiresome new breed of lawyers, Josh thought, teetotal as well as everything else. They settled at a table in the corner and ordered the Wig and Pen's traditional steak and oyster pie.

'It was good of you to meet me,' Michael said.

'No problem,' said Josh, 'I had to come up to London on business anyway,' he lied.

'I wanted to talk to you about Mel Paradise.'

'I rather thought you might,' said Josh.

'Do you know where she is at the moment?' Michael asked.

'Yes, she's down in St Ives staying with her mother.'

'So she hasn't approached you for a job? I rather thought she might.'

'Not so far,' said Josh. 'I think it might be a little hard for her to do so and rather claustrophobic. I'm her godfather and the firm is a small one and rather parochial compared with what she is used to.'

'It was me who messed things up, I'm afraid.'

'In what way?' Josh asked.

'We had a fling, Mel and I, soon after she joined the firm,' Michael toyed with the fork, 'it was a terrible mistake, obviously, I'm married but she is a very beautiful girl and …'

'You don't have to explain yourself to an old sinner like me,' said Josh. Michael looked up and smiled at him gratefully. Suddenly he looked less formidable and Josh warmed to him. 'Anyway,' said Michael, 'when it came to the question of Mel having the tenancy, she broke things off. She said that if we were going to work together in the long term, then an affair was inappropriate. She's right, of course, it was a very mature attitude.' He hesitated. 'My marriage isn't that good and I took it badly. Mel knew our relationship had no future so she wanted out.' He sighed, 'Josh you're not going to tell anyone about this are you?'

'No,' Josh said, 'no, of course not, Michael. I was just thinking actually, while I was waiting for you, I've known you since you were a baby. It would be a gross act of disloyalty to start blabbing about what you've just told me, besides which, as I told you, Mel is my goddaughter.'

'It's just that it was your indiscretion that finally put the kybosh on everything.'

'What do you mean?' Josh asked, frowning.

'You remember we met a few months ago and got hideously drunk as I recall – some family bash wasn't it?' Josh nodded. 'You told me then about old Charlie Paradise, how he had taken a bribe as a young man.'

'I told you that?' Josh said.

'I'm afraid so, old boy, you were very drunk. I think you have issues with Charlie, you seem to think he didn't rate you and yet all the time he had been carrying around this dark secret,' Michael hesitated. 'Maybe I will join you in a glass of burgundy, this tonic water tastes terrible.'

Josh smiled his relief and summoned the waiter. The men sat in silence for a moment or two until the glass of wine was delivered. Michael took a hefty swig. 'After all,' he said, 'I'm not due back in court again today.'

'Go on then,' said Josh. 'How does my indiscretion fit in with all this?'

'We had a row, Mel and I. I said I thought it was perfectly possible for two intelligent adult people to carry on a discreet affair without it disrupting the chambers in any way. She started moralising about me cheating on my wife and how our behaviour should be above reproach and how I should set a good example to junior barristers etc, etc and then she threw at me that her father had bought her up to have the highest possible moral code, so far as law and the practising of it is concerned. I was riled up, Josh, and out it came, that she shouldn't go quoting her precious father at me, he'd not been above taking a bribe or two in his youth, a far more serious offence than bonking a junior barrister.'

'You didn't say that.'

'I'm afraid I did,' said Michael.

'What, those exact words?'

'More or less.'

'What did Mel do?'

'She threw a book of law notes at me, rather a

heavy one actually and they really hurt – they caught me on the side of the ear.'

'Good,' said Josh, 'did she throw anything else?'

'No, mercifully,' said Michael.

'Pity.' A thought suddenly struck Josh and his face clouded. 'You didn't tell her how you knew about Charlie's bribes?'

'No I didn't,' said Michael. 'Give me some credit for not being a complete bastard. Mel asked me my source, of course, and I said I couldn't tell her. It was then that she told me not only to stuff our relationship but also the tenancy and several other things that would not have fitted up my dainty derrière. She stormed out of the room, cleared her desk and went, leaving me with a chinless wonder by the name of Jeremy Powell.'

Their steak and oyster pie arrived. 'So why are you telling me all this?' Josh asked.

'Because I feel bad about it. She is a hugely talented girl but she is her own worst enemy, she always says exactly what she thinks, irrespective of whether it is appropriate.'

'Refreshing though,' Josh suggested.

'Yes indeed, unless you happen to be on the receiving end. I thought you might be able to find her a job.'

'Surely you're better placed to do that Michael than me?'

'I'm nervous,' said Michael. 'I don't want to

appear to be taking too much interest in her in case the rumours start to fly. I think Fiona already smells a rat. She keeps asking why Mel left in such a hurry.'

'And I suppose meeting again might be painful for you both.'

'I don't think so,' said Michael, 'I don't think for either of us it was a serious love affair. Mel didn't have time for a boyfriend, I was there and convenient and she is an absolute corker in bed.'

'Please,' said Josh, 'she is my goddaughter. This is way too much information.'

'I'm sorry,' said Michael. 'So can you help?'

'I'll do my best but she has got to want a job first. From what her mother says she has just sort of opted out.'

'What on earth is she doing down in St Ives?' Michael asked.

'Painting a cottage as far as I can understand,' said Josh.

'Good God, I wouldn't have thought Mel knew how to hold a paintbrush.'

'I'll do what I can,' said Josh. 'Not to help you out but because I owe it to Mel and to Mel's family but I want your absolute reassurance that you will never tell Mel or anybody else how you knew about Charlie Paradise's bribe.'

'We have a deal,' said Michael, 'provide you tell no one of my affair with Mel.'

The two men shook hands solemnly.

9

Clara Gresham was about to go to bed. She had brushed her teeth, creamed her face and run the hairbrush through her hair fifty times like Nanny had taught her to do nearly sixty years before. Then wearily, she climbed into bed. Everything ached including her head, she had not slept properly in days. It was a terrible thing to lose a child, especially a troubled one such as her daughter who had experienced so little joy in her life – all wrong that a child should die before her parents. The pain of it made her heart palpitate – she would never have believed emotional pain could be so physical. It was particularly ironic that in the few days since Clara had learnt of her daughter's death, the awful years of Lizzie's alcoholism seemed to have vanished. All Clara could remember of her daughter, all that came into her mind when she thought of her, was of the charming, robust, good natured little girl she had been and the happy easy-going young woman she had become – or had become until she met Philip Hope. The twilight years that followed were shadowy. Clara now felt herself directly in touch with the young woman Lizzie had once been and this made her loss all the more poignant.

Suddenly, there was the sound of car tyres on gravel, headlights raked across her bedroom ceiling. There was a screech of brakes and the sound of the car engine was cut. For a moment, the silence of the countryside surrounding Juniper Farmhouse returned. Then a car door slammed. Who on earth would it be at this time of night ... and then with a sickening jolt Clara knew the answer to her own question. There was a hammering on the door, Clara clambered out of bed and put on her dressing gown. Should she telephone someone, the police, a neighbour? The police, were out of the question, of course – and then she heard his voice.

'Clara, Clara. Open up it's Philip. I know you're there. Open up or I'll break the bloody door down.'

If she stayed upstairs she would be trapped. She tiptoed down the stairs, running past the front door which trembled in its frame as the hammering continued.

'You might as well open up.' The voice sounded frighteningly close to her. 'I've got a key. You might just as well let me in Clara, I know you're in there and what I want to know what you've done with George. Where is he? I want the boy back and I want him now.'

She heard his feet on the gravel retreating

towards the car, obviously to get the door key. She had seconds. Where to hide? She ran to the kitchen, staring around her hopelessly, and then she thought of the tack room – the old outhouse which led directly from the kitchen. As noiselessly as she could and with trembling fingers, she drew back the bolt of the kitchen door. In the kitchen she'd had the benefit of the hall light, here she was in pitch darkness. She snapped on the light briefly to get her bearings. On top of the freezer, someone had left a horse blanket carelessly draped. She turned off the light, reached for the blanket and crouched down in a corner between the freezer and the wall, pulling the blanket over her as best as possible. It felt a pathetic gesture, the sort of thing a small child would do when playing hide and seek – ostrich-like, if I can't see him, he can't see me. He would find her, bound to. She heard the sounds of crashing doors inside the house and footsteps on the stairs. She tried to think of what clues she might have left as to her whereabouts. She had been lying in the darkness when he had arrived, there was no tell-tale bedside light; her own car was in the garage but Tom's was missing; maybe just maybe he would think the house was empty … and then she heard him come into the kitchen. There was another bang and the tack room door was flung open, light from the kitchen flooding in. She shrank into her corner. He must be standing in the doorway.

'Damn it, I don't know where you've gone but I'll find you. You can't hide from me.' The threat sounded very convincing to the shuddering figure under the horse blanket.

Then unbelievably, she heard his footsteps retreating across the kitchen floor. Moments later the front door slammed and the car engine started. Only when the sound of the car had disappeared into the night did Clara risk standing up. She was shaking from head to foot, itchy from the horse blanket. Trembling she went back into the kitchen and bolted the door.

There were two interesting factors which were confusing Keith Penrose. All his instincts told him that Lizzie Hope's murder was a crime of passion. However, while the bruising on her neck indicated that she had been strangled, the killer had worn gloves which in turn suggested that it was a premeditated act. Somehow it didn't stack up.

'It's so infuriating,' Keith grumbled to his sergeant. 'It was a marvellous piece of luck being able to identify the body – it could have been weeks before the Greshams realised their errant daughter was missing.'

'If the coastguards are right, what was she doing at out Malpas anyway, sir?' Jack asked.

'God knows,' said Keith, 'I suppose she could

have been going for a night-time stroll but it hardly seems likely. It seems more logical that she was lured there by her killer. It is a good spot for murder, I suppose.'

'And what was she doing in Cornwall anyway?' Jack asked.

'Looking for George?' the inspector suggested.

'You're confident that George really is in the Cornwall?' Jack asked.

'Mrs Paradise recognised him from the photograph and experience suggests that we have every reason to trust Mrs Paradise.'

'So if you believe her, sir,' Jack began, 'oughtn't we to be doing something about it?'

'I agree,' Keith said, a little tetchily. 'I'm just trying to work out whether we are justified in launching a full scale search for George. His father says he is with his grandparents, his grandmother says he is with his father, the neighbour of the grandparents has had no sighting of him and the neighbour of the father says he definitely went on a business trip with his father. However, the real point is we haven't clapped eyes on the boy.' Keith paused, stood up and wandered over to the window. 'In ordinary circumstances, I don't think we could justify police intervention. What makes this case different is that the little boy in question had a mother who has just been murdered, and he has been sighted by a reliable source, not twenty miles away from where the murder took place.' He swung around and looked Jack up and down. 'It's not unreasonable then to suppose that the boy could be in danger and that in any event he needs finding – right?'

'Right, sir,' said Jack, surprised. It was not like Keith to request verification of a decision – he was usually so definite about everything. 'So would you like me to rustle up some lads to give me a hand on a house to house? Where do you want to start – St Ives?'

Keith shook his head. 'I don't think we should start in St Ives, I think we should start in Zennor.'

'Okay, I'll get together a few of the boys and we'll be off. Could I have the photograph to make some copies?'

'Jack,' said Keith, 'have you ever been to Zennor?'

'Well, no, I don't think so,' said Jack.

'All that's needed for this job is you and I – trust me.'

The drive to Zennor took forty minutes. Jack Curnow drove and Keith sat huddled beside him in brooding contemplation. It wasn't until they were approaching the outskirts of St Ives that Jack finally plucked up the courage to ask the question that had been plaguing him during the last few weeks.

'Sir, I know it's none of my business but you've

not been yourself recently, and I just wondered whether there was anything I could do to help.'

'What do you mean 'not myself'?' Keith growled.

'Well sir, very uncommunicative and, well, rather short tempered and another thing – it's not like you to ask my opinion on what we should do next – you normally just do it. It's very disconcerting.' He stole a quick look at his boss – his expression was not encouraging.

'Cases involving children always upset me, you know that,' Jack nodded, 'and just at the moment …' Keith's voice trailed off.

'Just at the moment?' Jack said encouragingly.

'My daughter.'

'Carly?' Jack said.

Keith had forgotten that Jack had been at school with both of his children. He was older certainly, but not so much older that he didn't remember them.

'Yes Carly,' Keith confirmed. 'She has cancer, Hodgkin's Lymphoma, just been diagnosed. She's starting the treatment now.'

Having worked for Keith for over five years, Jack was well aware that his boss was a man of few passions. He had no time for hobbies, his marriage seemed to be centered around a sense of duty, his friends appeared to be work colleagues and apart from a few games of squash each month in a token attempt to keep fit, he lived and breathed for his job. The one exception to all of this was his children. He adored them both, was immensely proud of them and their achievements and appeared particularly close to Carly. For any parent a child with cancer was a nightmare, for his inspector … Jack literally shuddered at the wheel, trying to imagine what he was going through.

'I'm terribly sorry, sir, I just don't know what else to say.'

'It's alright, boy, there is nothing else to say,' Keith said gruffly, but not unkindly. 'She has a good chance of recovery, apparently but at the moment, well, she's going through hell with this treatment. Why her, why someone so young and so fit?'

'It's a terrible disease,' said Jack, 'and it seems to be reaching epidemic proportions.'

The two men were silent for a few minutes, lost in their own thoughts. Jack was thinking of his young cousin who had died of leukaemia. Keith, of course, was thinking of Carly.

'Turn left here,' said Keith, suddenly 'and just follow the road. I can't believe you've never been to Zennor.' It was a clear indication that the conversation on the subject of Carly was at an end.

Zennor is a magical place. Only six miles from St Ives, one enters a different world, a different time zone even. It consists of a church, a pub, a cluster of cottages, a wonderfully quaint museum, and apart from a few outlying farms, there is nothing surrounding Zennor but moorland and the sea. There is talk of mermaids, of shipwrecks and of smugglers – all of which seem suddenly quite believable to the casual visitor, unprepared for the very special atmosphere Zennor evokes. As the two policemen dropped down into the village that September morning, the heavy cloud cover with intermittent sunshine, gave the place a kind of brooding presence. They parked in the car park of the Tinners' which had yet to open for the lunchtime trade.

'I can see why you didn't think we needed help,' said Jack standing beside his boss, gazing around.

'Where do you want to start, sir? The pub?'

'No. Let's just take this row of cottages and work our way up the street. If they are here, we'll find them.'

The inhabitants of the first two cottages could not help. They had seen no sighting of the boy in the photograph. At the third cottage an old lady sat in the doorway topping and tailing a bowl of gooseberries.

'This looks more like it,' Keith said under his breath, 'an old granny who misses nothing.'

They introduced themselves, she studied the photograph of the boy for an unnecessarily long time, peering at it this way and that.

'I reckon he comes from one of those holiday

cottages up the hill,' she said, 'I think I've seen him with his grandpa.'

Keith's heart quickened. 'Have you seen him recently?' he asked.

'Last day or two, can't tell you when exactly, my boy. One day is much like another when you get to my age.'

'Well thank you very much indeed for your help,' said Keith, smiling.

Ten minutes later the two men knocked on the door of a tiny cottage set back from the road. The door was opened by a tall, imposing looking woman. She looked from one to the other, her face creased with dismay, mingled with something else – relief perhaps Keith thought.

'Ah, sergeant,' she said, recognising Jack. 'Sergeant Curnow isn't it?' She spoke as if they were meeting at a party.

'Yes, Mrs Gresham, that's right,' Jack said, 'this is Inspector Keith Penrose and this, sir, is George's grandmother, Clara Gresham.'

So full had his mind been with thoughts of his daughter that Keith had forgotten that it had been Jack that had taken Clara Gresham to identify her daughter's body. 'I'm sorry to trouble you, Mrs Gresham,' he said, 'at what must be a very difficult time but I wonder if we could talk to you for a few moments.'

'You'd better come in inspector,' Clara said, 'it's

a relief, in a way, that you've found us.'

'A relief?' Keith said, so he'd not been wrong.

Clara sighed. 'Come and meet my husband and we'll explain.'

The policemen followed Mrs Gresham into the cottage, Jack having to bend low under beams. A man in his late middle age was sitting by a cheerful fire reading *The Times*. He looked up as they entered and the colour drained from his face. He jumped up hurriedly, looking enquiringly at his wife.

'Tom, this is Inspector Penrose and his sergeant, Sergeant Curnow.'

'What is it you want now?' Tom Gresham said. 'As if we haven't enough to cope with at the moment with the death of our daughter.'

Keith studied the man in silence for a moment. He was probably in his early sixties, barely as tall as his wife, but thick set and strong. He looked ex-army – it was strange how men who had been in the services never lost the look even when they had been in mufti for years.

'I'm very sorry to trouble you, sir, but we're enquiring about the whereabouts of George, your grandson. He seems to have disappeared.'

'He hasn't disappeared,' Tom Gresham said, 'he's here with us.'

Clara moved across the room and closed the door to the little cottage staircase which led to the floor above. 'Ssh,' she said, 'not so loud. We don't want to upset him. He is finding life rather difficult at the moment. Why are you wanting to find him?'

'Because your son-in-law told us he was with you and you told us he was with your son-in-law.'

'Well that's hardly an issue, is it?' said Tom Gresham, still aggressive. 'You must have asked us both at different times. George spends quite a lot of time with us and obviously with his father and in any event, I really don't see what business it is of yours where George is.'

'In ordinary circumstances,' said Keith, patiently, 'I would agree with you, sir, but these circumstances aren't ordinary. I'm sorry not to be able to put this in any other way but the fact is your daughter was murdered just over a week ago and she is George's mother. In the circumstances, we would just like to reassure ourselves that George is well and safe with someone.'

'He is well and safe with us,' said Tom Gresham, 'now if you wouldn't mind leaving us in peace, we're trying to grieve for our daughter and comfort our grandson on the loss of his mother. We certainly don't need interruptions from the police.'

'Tom,' Clara said, 'please we've both had enough of this. It's time we explained to the police what's going on, it really is.'

Tom shot her a furious look. 'I don't know what you're talking about,' he said, 'nothing is going on.'

'We have a story to tell you,' Clara said to

Keith. 'If you and your sergeant would like to sit down, I will tell it to you, even if my husband won't. I'll just check on George and make sure he's happy playing for a while, I don't want him to overhear what we have to say.'

She opened the door to the stairs and ran up them, surprisingly agile for her age. Keith did as he was told and sat down on the chair opposite Tom Gresham.

'I really am sorry about this sir , but it is our duty to investigate every aspect of your daughter's murder and one of those aspects is to establish the whereabouts and welfare of your grandson.'

There was a cry from the top of the stairs, Clara came almost tumbling down it. Tom jumped to his feet. 'What is it? What is it?'

'He's not there,' Clara shrieked.

'What do you mean, he's not there?'

'For Christ's sake Tom, what else do I have to say. He's disappeared, he's not there, George isn't in his room.'

'He must have gone out into the garden,' Tom wrestled open the sitting room door which led onto a kitchen. He ran through the kitchen, his wife in pursuit. He fumbled with the kitchen door and went out into the garden. The two policemen followed.

'Are they taking the piss, sir ?' Jack whispered.

Keith shook his head. 'I don't think so, I think this is for real.'

The garden was a small square patch of rough grass with nothing to commend it, not even a flower bed. The very exposed grass was almost more like moorland than anything approaching a lawn. Its central feature was a rotating clothes horse on which Keith noted there hung a pair of boys' jeans and a couple of T-shirts. It would appear that even if George Hope wasn't here now, he had been.

Clara was turning to her husband. 'Where can he have gone, when did he go, where is he – oh, Tom?'

Tom shook his head helplessly. The couple were certainly in a very genuine state of agitation.

Keith stepped forward. 'When did you see the boy last?'

The couple stared at Keith and then at each other. There was no conspiracy here, Keith saw, they were just two desperate people.

'Breakfast, at breakfast,' said Tom, 'we bought him a new set of Lego, a complicated one, a pirate ship. He said he would do it upstairs in his room. He's spent quite a lot of time on his own since his mother died, it seems to suit him.'

'So he knows his mother is dead?' Keith said.

Tom nodded dumbly. 'And he found out in the worst possible way. We were renting a cottage in St Ives when the tragedy happened. I was making him a boiled egg for tea. I was in the kitchen and he was watching television. The six o'clock news came on, he normally switches over and watches the Simpsons but for some reason he didn't. When it came to the local news, there it was, news of a murder and you talking about it,' Tom said, looking at Keith, 'and then of course you showed the artist's impression. I came in just as they flashed it on the screen. We both knew it was her before my wife identified the body – it was a very good likeness. He's been very traumatised ever since. I just can't understand where he's gone.'

'We must search for him, we must search for him now.' Clara was wringing her hands.

'So how long is it since breakfast?' Keith asked.

'About an hour, I suppose,' said Tom.

'Well an eight year old can't get very far in an hour. Don't worry, we'll find him.'

'I'm going out to look for him now,' Tom said.

'No,' said Keith, 'come back into the house with me. Jack you have a quick scout around the village. If you can't find him in the next ten minutes get some back-up and put Culdrose on standby. We'll put up a helicopter if necessary, that's the quickest way to find him around here.'

10

George just couldn't stand any more shouting. He wondered if all adults shouted or whether it was just his family. As long as he could remember there had been shouting. His mother and father shouting at one another, his mother shouting at his grandparents and now the most horrible of it all, his grandparents shouting at one another. They had never done that before. The argument had started in the little sitting room below his bedroom and now they had taken themselves out to the garden, presumably so he wouldn't hear them. However, peering through the window of his bedroom he could see them below and although he couldn't hear what they were saying, he could see their angry gestures. It was just not like Granny and Gramps at all – they were normally smiley with each other. It was horrible, just horrible.

He made his decision immediately and with surprising ease. He was going to live in the wild. He would track rabbits, kill them and roast them; he could catch fish too and eat blackberries. No one would tell him what to do; it would be a fine life. Into his school bag he packed spare pants and socks, a T-shirt, his torch and the rug from the bottom of his bed. He looked at Teddy and very regretfully decided that he would have to stay behind. It was not an easy decision. He was already wearing his favourite army trousers and from his drawer, he found very satisfactorily his army jacket. He looked like a real soldier and he was going to lead a soldier's life. He began putting on his old trainers then he saw the new ones that Granny had brought him when she arrived yesterday. He should really wear the old ones because he would get them muddy, but since he wasn't coming back, he might as well wear the new ones. The thought frightened him and for a moment he stood paralysed after his violent burst of activity. What was he doing? He looked at the bed, Teddy was watching him reproachfully. In a flash he picked up Teddy, stuffed him unceremoniously into his school bag and began creeping down the stairs.

In the kitchen George raided the fridge, some yogurts and a bottle of orange juice; he found a packet of KitKats, an apple, a banana and in the kitchen drawer a sharp knife. He heard the sound of his grandparents coming back into the cottage, there was no time for anything more. He slipped out of the kitchen, into the hall and out of the front door. His bike was propped against the garage door. He was planning to go up onto the cliff path, to lead his new life up on Zennor Tor where he had been with Gramps. If he took his bike and biked along the lane to the cliff path, he would be quicker and everyone would think he had gone the other way up to the main road. That was a very clever thought. He adjusted his school bag as a back pack, jumped onto his bike and began pedalling through the village. He glanced over his shoulder. There was no one out at the front of the cottage, he had got away without his grandparents seeing him. He bicycled as hard as he could along the lane that led to a coastal path. When he reached the coastguard's house, he jumped off his bike and looked right and left. There was no one around. He pushed the bike up behind a stone wall and laid it on its side, then gathering pieces of bracken he began covering it. After five minutes of hard work, the bike was no longer visible. He looked at his handiwork, very pleased, no one would ever find it there. He wondered when he would ever see his bike again and once more he was enveloped by sadness. Still a soldier had to make tough decisions sometimes and this was a good one. The enemy would never find him and they would never find his bike. Squaring his shoulders he turned his back on the village and began clambering up the path that would lead him onto the coastal path to St Ives. The sun was high in the sky warming his back. He was free, no more shouting, no more arguments, he was his own man now, he would make his way in the world, he didn't need anyone. These thoughts put a spring in his step, he strode along whistling, confident he could beat his enemies whatever game they chose to play.

'And he's taken his bike,' Tom Gresham said, his voice rising in panic. 'I don't know whether he'll have gone towards St Ives but presumably he'll be on the road somewhere which will make him more difficult to spot, won't it?'

'Possibly,' Keith admitted, 'but don't worry, sir , I'm sure we'll find him. It's not difficult to spot a little boy on his own and with that colour hair he'll stand out like a sore thumb. We're putting the helicopter up now and back-up is on its way. We'll have the place crawling with officers in no time, we'll find him.'

While the men were outside, Clara had made a search of George's room. 'He's wearing his army things,' she said, 'he loves his army trousers and jacket, he's just at that age,' she smiled at Keith for the first time. She must have been a very beautiful woman once Keith thought, smiling back. All the iron control, Jack had told him about which she had displayed when identifying her daughter's body, had gone. She was just a very scared and clearly devoted grandmother. For a moment Keith imagined what it must be like to be Clara Gresham. She had lost her granddaughter and less than a week ago she had lost her daughter. Now her grandson was missing. It was a nightmare, he would have to go very gently.

'Did he take anything with him, Mrs Gresham?' he asked.

'Yes, he's taken his school bag, it's just a surfing rucksack.'

'What colour?' Keith asked.

'It's sort of cream and brown. He's taken a few clothes by the look of it and his rug and ...' her voice broke slightly, 'and Teddy, his teddy bear.'

Keith met her eye. 'In which case, he's serious about running away, isn't he?' There was no hint of a smile. For the first time Clara studied this kind, careworn man. She was very glad, suddenly, that Inspector Penrose was in charge of finding George.

'Yes,' she said, 'yes, inspector, you're quite right, of course.'

It was four o'clock and there was still no sign of George. They had conducted a house-to-house of every single property in the Zennor area, farm barns had been searched, there had been a road block set up in both directions, cars checked and motorists interrogated for any sign of George. There had not been a single sighting. The helicopter had combed backwards and forwards along the cliff path in both directions, they had spotted nothing. George Hope seemed to have disappeared off the face of the earth. The Greshams had joined in the hunt around the village, calling their grandson's name, becoming more and more exhausted and terrified. When there was still no sighting of him by four, Keith had insisted that they came back to the cottage, have a cup of tea and talk to him. While Clara made tea, Keith kindled some life into the fire and Tom fetched some logs. No one could eat anything.

'It's getting colder now,' Clara said, as her trembling hand poured the tea. 'Here we are sitting by this fire and he's out there somewhere. It'll be dark in a few hours, inspector.'

'We are doing everything we can to find him, you know that.'

'Yes, of course I know that, but it's not working, is it?'

'I think perhaps you'd better tell me what's really going on here,' Keith said.

Tom Gresham looked at him sharply. 'What are you saying? Are you trying to suggest that he's not really missing?'

'No, no, of course not, I know the boy has gone missing, but I need to know why. I also need to understand why everyone has been lying to us about his whereabouts. While we wait for news I think it's about time you told me exactly what has been going on in the last week or so, that has caused George's father to confirm that George is with you and for you to tell everyone that George was with his father. It doesn't make any sense to me, nor does it make any sense that so soon after the death of his mother, George's father doesn't see fit to be spending any time with his son.'

'That's not his fault,' Clara said. 'I can't stand the man, but it's not his fault he's not with George at the moment.'

'And why would that be?' Keith asked, accepting the teacup handed to him.

'Because we've kidnapped George, inspector, that's why we're stuck out here in this cottage – we're hiding.'

'From whom? Keith asked.

'Everyone,' Clara said, simply.

'So,' Keith said, 'are you going to tell me about it?' He glanced from one to the other. Tom Gresham's army bearing seemed to have collapsed. He had shrunk in the last hour or two, his face almost grey with fatigue. 'So which one of you is going to tell me what is really going on?' he asked gently.

'I will,' said Clara, after a moment. She took a deep breath. 'We never liked Philip. He is, was, quite a lot older than our daughter, she was only nineteen when they married and he was thirty-one. Quite frankly, inspector, he s a bully.'

'You mean he hit her?' Keith asked.

'No nothing like that, but he undermined her, zapped her confidence, he was always putting her down, even in public.'

'She was such a glorious girl,' Tom suddenly interjected. 'Young, strong, happy. She had the same blonde hair as George, oh ...' He paused for a moment, a look of horror crossed his face, 'You know that of course.'

Keith's mind flitted briefly to the body of the woman in the mortuary and glancing at Clara, he saw the same thought mirrored in her eyes, too. 'Oh God,' he thought, 'how can they bear this?' He pulled himself together with effort. 'So she wasn't drinking then, when she married Philip?'

'Good Lord, no,' said Clara. 'I mean she was a teenager, nineteen, she went to parties and I'm sure there were occasions when she drank too much, but no, she wasn't in any way an alcoholic.'

'So when did the drinking start?'

'It was slow, insidious,' she said. 'We became aware of it when the four of us went out together. If, for example, we went out for family meal to celebrate someone's birthday, we suddenly became aware that Lizzie was drinking a lot more than the rest of us, but in the beginning we never worried about it because we assumed it was an occasional thing and we understood why she did it. Philip was always criticising her about what she was wearing or what she had said, even I remember one evening, her table manners. It was appalling,' Clara glanced across at her husband, 'Tom and I couldn't bear it. When she was expecting Megan she seemed to improve. She took having a baby very seriously and was very careful with what she ate and also drank. When Megan was born …' again there was the break in Clara's voice. She hesitated, '… when Megan was born,' she began again, 'she was a devoted mother – the baby seemed to be just what she needed. She had someone to love and who loved her and even Philip couldn't criticise her mothering skills in the early days. Then they moved house and that's when things started to go wrong again. They had lived from the day they married in a cottage in Wooton, near Woodstock. It is friendly village and she knew everyone and other young mothers like herself. She was happy there, but Philip's business was doing well so he bought a huge old farmhouse near Chipping Norton. His business is based in Chipping Norton, I don't know if you're aware of that.'

Keith shook his head. 'What is his business?'

'He develops and sells computer software,' Tom said. 'He's very clever at what he does, I believe.'

'Is it the sort of business your daughter could have become involved in?'

'No, no, she was arty and absolutely hopeless with computers, or any such thing – a real technophobe. She had no interest in Philip's business and I suppose, in fairness, that must have been quite hard for him,' Tom said.

He was obviously making a huge effort to be fair. This is a nice couple, Keith thought. 'So Lizzie wasn't happy in the new house?' he asked.

'No, no it was too big and ...' Clara hesitated, 'Philip bought it for show, not because it was a lovely family home. He bought it after no real consultation with Lizzie and it was isolated, miles from anywhere, so instead of being able to push the buggy to the village shop she was all alone. I think he was jealous of her friends.'

'And so she started drinking again?'

Clara nodded. 'She was so lonely. When Megan was three, Philip insisted that she went to nursery school in Oxford.'

'To St Leonard's?' Keith asked.

Clara looked up in surprise. 'You've done your homework, inspector. Yes, yes to St Leonard's. Over the years that followed drink took its hold and then when Megan was eight, rather unexpectantly George was born.'

'Did she stop drinking again?'

'She certainly tried very hard for George and she got it under control I think, up to a point, but it was different from when Megan was a baby. The alcoholism had really taken its toll and got its grip. She certainly fought it, but it was always there.'

'Didn't she try to seek help, didn't you try to persuade her to get help?'

Tom let out an anguished wail. 'Oh, inspector,' he said, 'the times we have tried to get her into rehab, to persuade her to see people, but you know what they say about alcoholics, you can only help them when they are ready to help themselves and she has never been ready. We once got her to see a psychiatrist, a friend of ours, but she walked out on him after a couple of minutes.'

'So George's babyhood was perhaps not as good as Megan's?' Keith suggested.

'She loved both her children,' Clara said, defensively and then saw the expression on Keith's face and said, 'No, you're right, inspector, George's babyhood was more turbulent. By the time he was a year old, Philip had bought Mulberry House in Charlbury. He removed the children one Friday afternoon, installed them in Mulberry House with an au pair and it was Monday before Lizzie even realised they were missing.'

There was a silence while the three of them sat contemplating the implication of what Clara had just said. It was shocking, tragic – Keith shuddered inwardly.

'She fought him,' Clara said, after a moment, obviously having to force herself to continue the story. 'She went to court, we supported her as best we could. The farm was sold, we helped her buy a little flat in North Oxford where she lived, until she, she died. Have you been to her flat, inspector?'

'No, I read the report from Thames Valley Police. There was no indication that there had been any struggle or trauma at the flat – indeed it was extremely neat and tidy, surprisingly so perhaps.' There was no reaction from either parent to the observation, so he continued. 'We've obviously checked the flat for DNA and fingerprinting so that we have that information available if we need a match in the future.'

There was a knock on the door.

'Perhaps there's news,' Clara jumped up and ran to the door. It was Jack. 'Have you found him?' she cried.

'No, nothing at the moment, I'm afraid Mrs Gresham. Sir, could I see you a moment?' Jack looked anxious.

'Excuse me,' said Keith and followed his Sergeant out onto the lane. 'What's happened?'

'Nothing, sir, it's just been suggested that the coastguards should take a boat along the coast in case the boy has fallen into the sea. I didn't want to say anything in front of the grandparents.'

'Good idea,' said Keith, 'and thanks – you can be quite a tactful bugger when you think about it.'

'Thank you sir, I'll take that as a compliment. How is it going in there?'

'Awful,' said Keith, 'I'm just hearing the whole story now. I don't think they're attempting to keep anything from us. I haven't got to the bottom of it yet but it looks like they've taken the boy away from Philip because George is unhappy with his father.'

Back in the cottage Clara resumed the story.

'Lizzie and Philip were in and out of court over the next year or so. Philip won custody of the children and Lizzie was allowed access but was not allowed to drive them anywhere, which, of course, was sensible, and then ...,' she ran a hand through her hair, an elegant gesture, despite her agitation, 'and then came the day of the accident. Lizzie had been drinking. She just could not bear being separated from her children any longer. George was in a day nursery. We didn't like it; we had offered to look after him but I think Philip felt that if he was with us, he would probably have access to his mother and he didn't want that, so poor little George spent every day alone in a nursery. She went there first and picked him up.'

'And then went on to St Leonard's,' Keith said.

'You've read the file, obviously.'

'Yes,' said Keith.

'After the accident, after Megan died, Lizzie came to live with us. She was an absolute wreck and for a while she stopped drinking but when the court hearing was over she just couldn't cope with her daughter's death and she started drinking again. It was the final straw for Philip and I do see that, of course I do, I would be a monster if I didn't. Lizzie has only had occasional supervised access to George since the accident and has only seen him briefly, except for the last time.'

'What last time?' Keith asked.

168

'In May,' said Clara. 'It was George's eighth birthday. Philip had to be away on a business trip in Switzerland and very reluctantly agreed that we could have George on condition that Lizzie kept well away. We assured him that Lizzie wouldn't even know that it was George's birthday, and he came and spent a week with us. We had a lovely time, and on his birthday,' she hesitated, 'we invited his mother.'

Tom took over. 'We asked her over early in the morning, we told her that we were taking a terrible risk and that she had to make a real effort not to drink.'

'We just couldn't bear the idea that she couldn't see her son any more,' Clara said, 'and of course George was quite safe with us.'

Keith smiled at them both. 'Look you don't have to justify the decision to me. What happened?'

'It was marvellous,' Clara said. 'They had a wonderful day together.'

'Lizzie and George?'

'Yes,' Clara said. 'They got on so well. She had bought him an entirely appropriate present, it was an army tank, and he loved it. They played all day together and then she left. They both cried when they parted, it was terrible but terrible in a good way.' Keith nodded. 'Everything changed from that day,' said Clara. 'George was much happier in himself and …' she paused dramatically, 'Lizzie stopped drinking. From that day, May 26th, George's eighth birthday

169

until the day she died she never touched another drop, I'm sure of it.'

'But you say she never saw her son again?'

'No,' said Tom. 'That was the awful irony. Of course George went home and told his father that he had seen his mother and asked if he could see her again. Philip was absolutely furious, furious with us for allowing it. He saw it as a betrayal of trust, and of course he was right, but he has never made any real attempt to be a proper father to George. He is something of a cold fish, and so wrapped up in his work.' Tom looked at Keith. 'Have you met him inspector?'

'I have, sir .'

'Then I won't embarrass you by asking you what you thought of him, but he's not a very likeable man and he treats his son much, I suspect, like he treated his wife, and in the process he has undermined George's confidence. There have been a string of au pairs – he has never been prepared to pay for a permanent nanny or housekeeper to give George stability, although he could well afford it. After the birthday meeting, Lizzie decided to try and gain more access to George. She managed to acquire a doctor's report which indicated she had stopped drinking and she was in the process of going back to court with the hopes of having a little more access to him. We were obviously prepared to offer to take responsibility for George for whatever limited contact the court felt was appropriate for Lizzie. Philip was preparing to fight it all the way,' said Tom, 'and then he went on the business trip to Frankfurt.'

'We were having supper, it was just over two weeks ago and the phone went. It was George, he was crying. He had come back from school on the bus and there was no one at home. His father was away and the au pair seemed to have disappeared. She had a boyfriend and George reckoned she must be with him. The boyfriend had been staying over since his father was away and clearly George was longing for proper care. So,' said Clara, 'we got in the car and we drove over to Mulberry House. We left a message for the au pair in case she turned up – she still hadn't arrived although it was half past nine at night – collected George and left.'

'Then what happened?' Keith asked.

'We took him home for the night, he was exhausted poor child, and in the morning we made a plan. We knew that Philip would be coming back from his business trip at the end of the week and that he would demand George back. We talked everything through with George – he really was a very unhappy boy who hardly saw his father. He was longing to see his mother again, and was just so lonely, so starved of real affection.'

'I took him away on holiday,' said Tom, 'Clara stayed behind to hold the fort and I took him down to St Ives. We telephoned Lizzie and she was on her way down by train to meet us, but for some reason decided to get out at Truro, rather than come on to St Ives.' There was a poignant silence in the room.

'So,' said Keith, 'you decided to hang on to George.'

'Something like that,' said Tom. 'He had just lost his mother he was in a terrible state, poor boy, we couldn't hand him back to his father who, without doubt, would have been unkind about his mother and upset him still further. So George and I went to ground here in Zennor and when things became difficult and Philip started hassling Clara, she ran away and joined us.'

'How do you mean 'hassling?' Inspector Penrose asked sharply.

'He turned up one night,' Clara shuddered at the memory. 'He was trying to find George. I was frightened, I hid and he went away. I know we can't go on like this, I know we can't keep the boy from his father. It's just such an awful situation.'

'I can see that, but what is the plan for the future?'

Clara shook her head. 'I don't know inspector,' she said, wearily. 'We were just trying to help George come to terms with losing his mother, we couldn't think beyond that. I know there is no way we can keep him, not while his father wants him, we were just taking one step at a time. Tom and I just couldn't agree on what to do next.' She looked out of the window for a moment and then at her watch. 'Oh my God,' she said, 'it's nearly five and still no news. Inspector, what are we going to do?'

'Can I ask you just one question,' Keith said, 'and then I'll go and find out how the search is going.' The couple nodded in unison. 'Can either of you think of any reason why your daughter might have been murdered or who would want to kill her?'

'Well, yes,' said Tom, 'I can well understand Philip wanting her dead but I can't see how he could have done it, he was in Frankfurt.'

There was a silence in the room. Keith looked at Clara. 'Did she have any boyfriends?'

'I've been through all this with Thames Valley Police,' Clara said. 'Did they send you the report?'

'Yes they did,' said Keith. 'I got the impression of a rather lonely young woman, would I be right?'

'Yes, you would,' said Clara. 'When you are fighting a battle with alcoholism it's all encompassing. You have to concentrate very hard on it – if you take your eye off the enemy for one moment, it comes back with a vengeance and gets you again. She'd no real friends for years of course, just the other drunks she met in pubs around Oxford. She had insulted most of her true friends long ago, during drinking binges, and of course most people dropped her after Megan died. Nobody wanted anything to do with a woman who had killed her own daughter.'

'Thank you,' said Keith. 'You stay where you are and I will be back to you shortly. You do realise, don't you, that we will have to inform Philip Hope of his son's disappearance.'

Felicity was on the coastal path. She had walked up to Clodgy from St Ives. It was such a beautiful afternoon and she had found a sunny patch and had been sketching, leaning against a rock. Most conveniently, a fishing boat was down below her and she was using it as a model to draw the climax of her seagull story – the moment when the seagull appears out of the storm and leads the disorientated fisherman back into the safety of the harbour. Her drawing was going well. The season had ended and there were few walkers around and those who passed her, mercifully, didn't ask to see what she was drawing. She became aware of a fairly constant buzzing overhead and noticed that a helicopter appeared to be making a search of the coastal path. Idly at first she wondered who they were looking for, hoping that there had not been an accident. After a while the helicopter began to upset her, something was nagging at the back of her mind, something was wrong. The heat had gone out of the sun. Sighing, she packed up her sketchpad and on putting it away in her bag noticed her mobile. On instinct she picked it up and dialled Keith Penrose's mobile number. He answered almost immediately. He sounded out of breath as if he was running or walking hard. She could hear the sound of the wind slapping against his phone. A sense of foreboding overwhelmed her.

'I'm really sorry to trouble you inspector,' she said, 'but have you found George yet?'

'Hang on one moment, Mrs Paradise, let me just catch my breath.' There was the sounds of scrabbling and then the wind had quietened. 'That's better,' he said, 'I'm just sheltering underneath a rock.'

'Where are you?' She asked curiously.

'I'm at Zennor,' he said.

'You're looking for George, aren't you?' She said, her voice shrill with tension.

'Yes, we are,' he said, 'how did you know?'

'I just did,' she said, 'I can't believe he's still missing?'

'We found his grandparents in Zennor village, but it appears that George has run away. We don't think he's up on the Tor, we think he's taken off by road because his bike has gone. I've just left the grandparents to see how the search is progressing – nothing yet.'

'Is that what the helicopter has been doing all afternoon?' Felicity asked, anxiously.

'Yes,' said Keith.

'And you say you've found nothing, not a sighting?'

'Not so far. Look I'll have to go, Mrs Paradise, I'll keep you posted, I promise.'

After Keith cleared the line, Felicity sat motionless for some minutes. Her mind was awash with emotion – the knowledge that George, like his sister before him, was now in danger, appalled her. She felt sick with apprehension, her heart heavy, her limbs numb, she felt incapable of movement. And then it came to her – one simple, lucid, clear thought – and without a moment's hesitation, she was suddenly and completely invigorated. She stood up, adjusted her bag over her shoulder and turning her back on St Ives, began walking up the hill towards the coastal path and Zennor.

George had spent rather an exciting day. He had scrambled up onto the cliff path and although once or twice, he had lost it, he had followed it, more or less, scrambling over rocks, sliding about in mud unless, of course, he saw people. When he saw people he hid because for all he knew they were the enemy. He enjoyed this game very much. He could see people coming from quite a distance and he kept a look out both in front of him and behind. He had one near miss with a couple who had a spaniel dog. He clambered off the footpath in good time, hid behind a rock and pulled his blanket over him which was brown and good camouflage. The people didn't see him, of course, but the dog found him and did a lot of wagging and barking at him.

'Come on, Sally,' the people called.

'What's she barking at?' the woman said to the man.

'Oh, it'll just be a rabbit, take no notice of her. If we keep walking she'll catch us up.'

George, frozen with fear, thought he would be discovered but he needn't have worried. Sally soon got bored with him and went running off after her owners. Other than Sally, it was no problem at all avoiding people and then during the afternoon, there was the helicopter. That was really good fun. The helicopter was looking for someone. George pretended that the helicopter was looking for him. He knew, of course, it wasn't really, but it was fun to pretend. The helicopter made sweeps up and down the cliff, flying quite low, but he had no problem hiding from it. He had plenty of time to find a good place each time it came because it made such a noise. Every time he heard the helicopter coming, he just hid behind a rock and pulled the blanket over him. It was easy to hide from the enemy – except for Sally, of course.

When he finished his orange juice, he carefully filled the bottle again from a rushing stream that he crossed. He was quite pleased with this, thinking it showed good survival skills. Altogether it had been a good day except that now it was getting dark and he knew he was lost – not that it mattered because he wanted to be lost, he wanted to get away from all the arguments, but he was worried about food. He had eaten the yogurt and the biscuits long ago, he had also eaten the apple and now all that was left was the banana. He had found a few blackberries which were rather hard and red and he hadn't enjoyed at all. Apart from that there had been no other food he could gather. Now, up here, the idea of killing and eating a rabbit just seemed disgusting. He also realised he had no matches so he didn't know how he would light a fire and cook the rabbit. Raw rabbit was not an option and anyway he hadn't seen one all day, let alone try and catch one. He had seen a mouse scuttling into the grass as he walked along the footpath and he had caught a glimpse of what he hoped very much was a grass snake and not an adder. Neither of these seemed very appealing to eat.

As darkness fell, he stumbled a couple of times over the rocks. He was tired now and he knew he was very near the edge of the cliff which frightened him. He could hear the sound of the sea crashing far below him and shuddered at the thought of accidentally falling over the cliff. The wind was getting up too and making him cold. Ahead of him was a strange pile of rocks and he sat down by them for a moment to consider what to do next. As he lowered himself on to the ground he realised that he was sheltered from the wind and suddenly it seemed like a good place to sleep. Solemnly he ate his banana and drank all the water, then he unpacked his blanket and Teddy and using his bag as a pillow, tentatively he lay down. It was actually quite comfortable.

George lay for some time listening to the sound of the sea way below him and the wind moaning in the background. It was quite dark now. Out of the shelter of the wind, he was warm enough but he did feel scared. The enemy could be anywhere, there could be a bad man up here who would murder him like the bad man who had murdered Mummy. He thought he heard a sound and sat up, his heart beating, but it was nothing. In his head he counted how many people he had seen during the day – nine and the dog Sally. That was not very many people in a whole day and surely there would be nobody here now. He took a deep breath to stop his heart racing, shut his eyes and began to feel sleepy. As he lay there trying to sleep a terrible sadness started to well up in him. It began in his tummy and ended up in his throat and he began to cry, great big sobs he couldn't stop. He cried for a long time holding Teddy very tight and when exhausted he finally slipped into sleep; his last conscious thought was that he wanted his mother.

Mel couldn't understand it, it was half past seven and there was no sign of her mother. She had tried her mobile but it appeared to be switched off.

She hunted around in the fridge and found some chicken breasts and cooked them and mashed some potato, conscious and slightly guilty of the fact that this was the first meal she had prepared for her mother, since arriving in St Ives. She had been very spoiled over the last couple of weeks. The thought made her feel even more guilty about the various outbursts with which she had indulged herself and by eight o'clock, not only was she full of guilt and remorse, she was also extremely worried. Slipping on her coat she walked around the corner to Cormorant Cottage. Annie was in the kitchen feeding Martin what appeared to be a very fragrant steak and kidney pie.

'Hello, my bird,' said Annie, cheerfully. 'What can we do for you?'

'You haven't seen Mum, have you?' Mel asked.

'No, my girl, not all day.'

'She said she was going sketching this morning but she would be back in time to cook supper but it's eight o'clock and there's no sign of her.'

'Tried her mobile?' Martin suggested between mouthfuls, clearly the pie was too delicious to take precedence over Felicity's disappearance.

'Yes, it's switched off or out of battery or something, she's not replying anyway.'

Annie dried her hands on a towel and leant back against the Aga, studying Mel silently for a moment.

'It's not like her,' she agreed, 'she's a good girl, your mother, she wouldn't want to worry no one. I wonder where she'll be?'

'As soon as I've finished this,' Martin said between mouthfuls, 'shall we go and have a look around the town, she might be in the pub or something?'

'I don't see her out boozing on her own, it's not her style,' said Mel.

'She may have met someone,' Martin suggested, 'forgot the time, you know, it happens.'

'It's not the sort of thing Mum does,' Mel said.

'Well have you got any better suggestions?' Martin asked, amiably enough.

'No, not really, unless I suppose we contacted the police.'

'Oh come on,' said Martin, 'be reasonable. Your mother is normally home to cook your supper at seven. It's now eight o'clock and you call the police – I don't think so.'

'There's no need to be so sarcastic,' said Mel. 'I can't help being worried. I've already lost one parent, I don't want to lose the other.'

Martin laid down his knife and fork. 'I'm really sorry,' he said, 'give me five minutes and we'll mount a search.'

Annie had been watching this exchange with some interest. There was a spark between the two of them, that was obvious, the way they were unsettling one another. 'I'll tell you what, my bird, I'll pop round to Jericho Cottage and if you give me your mobile number, I'll call you if your mother either turns up or rings in – that way you won't go wasting your time, if there's no need.'

Mel looked extremely grateful. 'Thanks Annie, that's really kind of you.'

Martin stood up and reached for his coat. He bent over and kissed the top of Annie's head. 'And highly practical too, as always, bless you.'

By nine o'clock Mel and Martin had searched all the bars. No one had seen Felicity and certainly there was no sign of her. Annie hadn't rung. At the Sloop Martin suggested they have a drink.

'I can't sit drinking while Mum's missing.'

'It might relax you a little,' said Martin, 'a quick one will do us no harm.'

So they sat outside as the tide crept across the sand and the harbour lights reflected in the water. It was a beautiful setting and in any other circumstances Mel would have thoroughly enjoyed it. As it was a strange sense of unease had overtaken her. 'I'm going to have to do something if she's not back by the time I get home,' she said.

'Are you sure she didn't tell you she was going somewhere and you've just forgotten?' Martin suggested.

'No, of course not,' said Mel, 'I'm a lawyer, I

remember things.'

Martin laughed. 'I bet you're quite a scary one at that.'

Mel managed a smile, 'I can be.'

'So what are you going to do with the rest of your life, Mel?

'I really don't know,' Mel said, 'I just haven't a clue. I can't have been through all those years of study and training to give up the law but I feel disillusioned by it, I've lost my way.'

'Maybe you should do something else for a while,' Martin said. 'You can always go back to it.'

'Not if I want a decent job, not really, I need to stick with it.'

'And do you want a high-powered career?' he asked.

'I was aiming to be a QC, that was my dream.'

'Which was more than your father achieved,' Martin said, mildly.

'What's that supposed to mean?' Mel asked.

'Nothing, just an observation. I just wondered if that was what was driving you – doing better than your father.'

'No, of course not,' said Mel. 'I'm doing this for me.'

'Do you enjoy it, the practising of the law?'

'I'm good at it,' Mel said, frowning in concentration, 'and you usually enjoy things you're good at, don't you, so, yes, I suppose I do. I'm very good at detail, I am what you would describe as meticulous.' She grinned at Martin. 'That sounds rather pompous, doesn't it?'

'No, it's good to know your strengths,' he said, 'so you'd be wasted, for example, as a sous chef at the Seafood Café.'

Mel smiled. 'I would produce very meticulous dishes.'

They both laughed and as quickly as it came, the humour left her face. 'Dear God Martin, it's nearly ten. Let's go home and see if Annie's heard anything.'

Annie was waiting for them in the kitchen.

'No news?' Mel asked.

Annie shook her head.

'Your brother rang for a chat but I didn't say anything to him, I didn't see there was any point in worrying him.'

'Why not try her mobile again,' Martin suggested.

Mel searched in her coat pocket. 'Nothing,' she said after listening for a moment.

'Let me try,' said Martin. He redialled the number. 'It's not picking up,' he said, 'I would think she's out of battery.'

'So what shall we do?' Mel said, looking from one to the other.

'I don't know, my bird,' Annie said, 'but I think it's probably about time we started to worry.'

The object of so much anxiety was in a pickle of her own making. Felicity had defied all the rules of common sense and she knew it. On many occasions throughout her life she had been the victim of her own spontaneity – this time, she had really excelled herself. The moment she heard that George Hope was missing, she knew where he was; she knew he was up on Zennor Tor and that the police were wrong to believe he was anywhere else. Such was the nature of her relationship with Keith Penrose, that had she confided this piece of information to him, the chances were he would have taken her seriously and changed the direction of the search, she saw that now. She had been very stupid. Even if she had decided to search for George alone, then the sensible thing would have been to go back home, leave a message to say where she was, put on her walking boots and warm clothes, take water and some food and above all, charge her mobile. As it was, she had done none of those things. As soon as she had received the call from Keith – the last before the battery on her mobile died on her – she had left Clodgy and headed on the coastal path towards Zennor, dressed in jeans, an old pair of deck shoes and mercifully, as it turned out, a thick padded jacket.

It had been dusk by the time she reached the halfway point, or rather what she considered to be the psychological halfway point – a signpost which showed St Ives 3.5 miles in one direction and Zennor 3 miles in the other. Although in theory, Zennor was now nearer than St Ives, the path ahead was treacherous and difficult. With darkness approaching and armed with no torch, the sensible thing would have been to strike off across the fields to Zennor but that would mean leaving George alone up on the Tor and she just couldn't do that. Briefly the image of the Tinners' Arms came into her head. She thought of the roaring log fire, hot food and convivial company. She looked around her. There was, of course, no one in either direction on the cliff path as far as the eye could see. It was very beautiful but it was also, at this time of the evening, a very desolate place. The cliffs towered around her like great cathedrals, seagulls swooped and shouted to one another. Why did seagulls need so little sleep, Felicity wondered? They were so hyperactive – all other self-respecting birds would be safely tucked up on a nice cosy branch by now. She shuddered slightly. Nature was somewhat overwhelming in these circumstances, at this time of day. If this was how she was feeling, it was not hard to imagine how intimidated an eight year old might feel. There wasn't really a decision to make – she simply had to press on towards Zennor.

About half a mile further on, she tripped. It was not a bad fall. She grazed her knee and her ankle felt a little sore, but as she fell forward, she realised she was perilously near the edge of the cliff. She could hear the sea crashing way below her. This is stupid, she thought. It was a dark cloudy night, no moon, no stars to be seen, nothing to guide her but the sound of the sea and the great inky black shapes of the cliffs around her. She would have to stop, she realised that. Gingerly, she climbed off the path, away from the cliff edge. Feeling her way, she clambered up some rocks and found a little hollow out of the wind. She sat down and rested her back against the rock – it was far from comfortable. I'm too old for this sort of thing, she thought. She was hungry and thirsty but mercifully not cold. The cloudy skies had ensured a warm night. She shut her eyes and focused on George. She was near him she knew that, not terribly near, probably not within shouting distance but not far away. He was safe, for the moment, and he was sleeping, she could sense that. The trick would be to get to him in the morning before he started to move about. Her eyelids felt heavy, her head slightly swimmy and she had the beginnings of a headache – dehydration she supposed. It was the beginning of a long fitful night.

Keith Penrose arrived home that evening in a towering temper. He had just spoken to Philip Hope for the second time. He had telephoned him first while Philip was still at work. As George's father he needed to be informed once it became obvious that

George was missing and was not going to be that easy to find. On his way back to Truro Keith had phoned him again to say that they had called the search off for the night and would resume it at day break the following morning.

'Thank you inspector,' Philip Hope had said. 'I have a very important meeting first thing tomorrow morning. I will come straight down to Cornwall once it's over.'

'I thought maybe you'd want to travel down overnight, sir, to be here for the morning.'

'Inspector, there is nothing I can do that you are not already doing. I'm sure George will be fine, he's a sensible boy. He's obviously taken himself off on some boyish adventure and then got lost. He'll turn up.'

'His grandparents are worried sick,' Keith said.

'Then his grandparents should have thought twice about taking him away from his home when my back was turned. I am thinking of pressing charges – it was kidnap, they had no right to take him without my consent.'

'They believed what they were doing was in George's best interest, sir,' Keith had said.

'And in that,' Philip had said, 'they were clearly wrong.'

The man was an unpleasant piece of work. Even without knowing what Clara and Tom Gresham had told him about Philip Hope, Keith would have found the man's reaction extraordinary. It was impossible to believe that his boy could be missing and that he was going to put a business meeting ahead of coming to help in the search. Poor old George, it must be tough for him – his mother and sister dead and being stuck with such a cold fish of a father; no wonder he had run away. If his father wasn't worried, Keith mused as he pulled into his driveway, then he was probably doing the worrying for the two of them. Unhappy children did silly things. Had he accepted a lift from a stranger before road blocks were set up? It was quite possible, in which case George could be hundreds of miles away by now in the company of God knows who. Keith shuddered.

Barbara and Carly were in the kitchen and it sounded as if they were arguing. Carly was sitting at the kitchen table with a cup of tea and Barbara was hovering over her.

'There you are,' said Barbara, briskly, 'would you like your supper now, Keith. It's dried up of course but I suppose I can heat it in the microwave?'

Keith shook his head. 'No thanks. A cup of tea and a biscuit will be fine.'

Carly looked up and smiled at him. 'You're very late Dad?'

'I've got a missing boy up at Zennor.'

'What sort of age?' Carly asked.

'Eight.'

'Do you think he's been abducted?' Carly asked.

'I don't know,' said Keith, 'I've just been mulling over that possibility as I was driving home.'

'Did he run away from home or was he taken?'

'He ran away,' said Keith. He sat down wearily. 'It's rather a long and complicated story but essentially I suspect he's a very unhappy boy.'

'And you don't have a clue where he is, what a nightmare, Dad!'

'No not a clue.'

'Where's Jack?' Barbara asked.

'Still out there,' said Keith. 'He's going to grab a few hours sleep at the Tinners', but we've kept him and a young constable at the scene in case there's any developments.'

'That'll please Maggie,' Barbara said, putting a cup of tea and some biscuits down in front of Keith.

Maggie was Jack Curnow's new wife who had a high disregard for the police force, bearing in mind the amount of time it took her husband away from her.

'I expect she'll settle down,' Keith suggested.

'I doubt it,' said Barbara, 'not that one. Jack will have to make a decision sooner or later – his career or his wife.'

'Like me,' said Keith with a grin, trying to lighten the mood.

'Like you,' said Barbara, 'you made your decision long ago, you chose your career when we were hardly back from our honeymoon.'

There was a nasty pause. Keith risked a glance at Carly and was rewarded with a cheeky grin.

'What have you been doing today then?' he asked Carly, anxious for a change of subject.

'Not puking, Dad. I haven't been sick once, in fact I'm feeling a lot better.'

'But she won't eat anything,' Barbara interjected, 'nothing. I've tried all day to get her to take something, but she won't. She's never going to build up her strength if she doesn't start eating.'

'Leave the girl alone,' Keith said, 'her body knows best. She'll start eating again when she is good and ready.'

'And what would you know about it? It's very important she has good nourishment at the moment – it's absolutely vital. It could make all the difference to the outcome.'

'Could I say something?' Carly said. Her voice was strained and Keith instantly regretted his outburst. 'If you two want to help me,' she said, 'the very best thing you can do is to ignore the cancer. I just want life to be as normal as possible. I don't feel like eating at the moment, Mum, so I'm not going to, but when I do, I will. I don't want to talk about my treatment or the prognosis or when I can go back to work or when my hair will start growing again. I just want to take one day at a time, and live it like nothing has happened.'

'I'm only trying to do what's best for you,'

Barbara said, grumpily.

'I know you are and I appreciate it,' said Carly. 'I just don't want to turn this, this illness of mine into a big drama. I want everything to be as normal as it possibly can.'

'In which case,' said Barbara, 'I'll go to bed. It's way past my bedtime anyway. Don't keep her up now, Keith, she needs her sleep.'

'I think you should give up sport and think about a career in the diplomatic corps,' Keith suggested when they heard Barbara's footsteps overhead.

'I don't think so, Dad, I've upset Mum now, but do you understand?'

'I think so,' he said, 'you're not in denial, you just don't want to talk about it and think about it all the time.'

'And it's not that I don't appreciate all the care and attention you're both giving me, it's just …'

'Suffocating,' Keith suggested.

'Exactly and I want to think about ordinary things. I want to think about going to the cinema and meeting some mates and buying some new clothes now I've lost so much weight. I have to fight this thing in my own way, Dad. Mum has been great, don't get me wrong, but she's turning it into a career. She's read everything there is to read about it on the internet. She's got diet sheets, exercise programmes, everything you can imagine, you know how ruthlessly efficient she is. She means well, of course, but you're right, it's suffocating. I know the very best solution is to get back to just being me, between now and the next bout of treatment.'

Keith reached out a hand and took Carly's in his. Her hand felt very fragile and it made his heart turn over in his chest. 'I'm very proud of you, you know that.'

'Yes, I do Dad.'

'You just do what feels right for you and don't worry about us. I'll sort your mother out, if need be.'

'And that's another thing,' Carly said, 'how come you and Mum are so grumpy with one another these days?'

'Are we?' Keith asked, genuinely surprised.

'Yes, all you ever do is snap at one another.'

Keith considered the question in silence for a moment. 'I suppose you and your brother were always what bonded us together. With you two gone, your mother and I rattle around a bit, bump into each other's sharp corners, rub each other up the wrong way.'

'You just seem so far apart,' Carly said.

'Well I suppose we are. As usual, I am spending too much time at work and your mother is so tied up with her duties with the Planning Authority. I don't think she's terribly interested in what I do and to be frank, Carly, I'm really not at all interested in what she does. We haven't got much common ground except for you children.'

'That's sad after, how many years of marriage?'

'Thirty-two,' Keith said.

'You're not always going to be a policeman and she's not always going to have a job in planning. You ought to start thinking about retirement, mend some bridges, find some things you do have in common, or once you stop working, life's going to be a bit bleak.'

'Retirement is something I can't even contemplate,' Keith said, trying to ignore the sense of panic which always accompanied the thought of no longer doing his job.

They had done some searching. Martin had been up to Barnoon car park and established that Felicity's car was there; her walking boots were still at home, so she hadn't intended to go far. Her handbag and money were in the cottage – in fact, all that was missing was her coat and her sketch pad. It was after midnight now and there appeared to be nothing more that the three of them could do.

'I think we should report her missing to the police,' Mel said.

'I don't,' said Martin, 'not until the morning. There is nothing they can do now anyway.'

'Annie, what do you think?' Mel asked.

'The same,' said Annie, 'but in the morning I don't think we should just ring the police, I think we should ring Inspector Penrose.'

'If we can find him,' Martin said, 'ringing the police these days normally means talking to some copper the other side of the country.'

'No problem there,' said Annie. 'I have his mobile number.'

'Do you now,' Martin said, with a smile. 'You are a dark horse.'

'Felicity gave it to me,' Annie said, primly, 'I have it safe at home. Let's give him a ring at seven o'clock tomorrow morning if there is still no sign of her.'

'She could be hurt somewhere, lying in the dark, seriously ill, anything.' Mel's voice rose in panic.

'She's alright,' said Annie, 'bad news always travels fast – no news is just that Mel, my bird, it's no news.'

Clara and Tom Gresham couldn't go to bed. Tom made up the fire and they sat in chairs opposite one another, occasionally drifting off into sleep, only to jerk awake again in panic.

'I don't understand how he got out of the cottage without us hearing him?' Clara said, for about the umpteenth time.

'It would have been easy,' Tom replied yet again. 'We were so busy shouting at one another, a herd of elephants could have marched out of the house and we wouldn't have known.'

'Is that why he went, because of the shouting?' Clara said in a small voice.

'I think so,' said Tom, 'we behaved very badly, I'm afraid. We knew he was in a state, losing his mother and before that being left alone by his father. We just took it for granted that he wanted to be with us no matter what, because it's what we wanted so much. We didn't consider how we should behave at all – it was very arrogant of us.'

'I think he is happy to be with us,' said Clara. 'It's just that he's had rather a lot of shouting in his life and it's the one thing we never do, do we, Tom – not normally.'

Tom nodded in agreement. 'Poor old boy, when we get him back, we'll promise him it won't happen again, and it won't, will it?'

'If we get him back,' Clara said.

'We will, don't worry.'

'But what will happen now, Tom? After this, Philip is never going to let us near George again and with Lizzie gone, I just can't bear it.' Clara began to sob and Tom eased himself stiffly out of his chair and went and knelt beside her, slipping his arms around her awkwardly. 'What terrible thing did we ever do in our lives, Tom, to deserve all this? First we lose our daughter to that awful man and drink, then we lose Megan, then Lizzie dies, murdered, I can't believe she's been murdered and now George is missing. Not many more terrible things can happen to us.' She almost wailed in her despair and Tom held her closely. He couldn't think of anything positive to say.

She woke to the sound of a yelp of pain. After seconds of absolute confusion as to where she was, she realised that the sound, in fact, had come from her own lips. Everything hurt, her back, her hips, her head, her shoulders. She struggled to her feet every muscle and joint seemed rock solid with stiffness and she was cold too, cold through to the bone.

'When did I grow this old?' Felicity said out loud, shaking and waggling her arms and legs, in a warm up exercise, a throwback to her days on the school lacrosse field more years ago than she could dare contemplate at this moment.

It was still essentially dark but there were grey streaks in the sky and unlike the darkness that had defeated her the previous night, there was much less density to it. Certainly it was safe to walk along the cliff path, with caution. It could only be just over two miles now to Zennor, and despite her appalling night and her aches and pains, Felicity felt strangely energised. 'I'm going to find you George, if it's the last thing I do,' she thought to herself and with the thought came a surge of confidence which had her swinging her bag over her back and cautiously climbing down onto the cliff path. It was hard going, up and down hill, slippery, slimy rocks covered in mud, puddles at every turn. There would be a few yards of straightforward path and then suddenly up would rear a great mound of rock, which had to be negotiated with great care, or else the path would plunge treacherously downwards, only to climb steeply again a few yards further on. It was not the moment to break an ankle.

So progress was slow. At this point on the Tor there were plenty of streams and after a while Felicity stopped and splashed water into her face, rubbing the sleep out of her eyes. She instantly felt much better. She didn't know what she was looking for quite – his blonde head or perhaps some brightly coloured children's clothing. The cliff stretched out ahead of her and behind her and seemed so vast, such a huge place in which to find one little boy. He could be anywhere and yet she knew he wasn't, she knew she was heading towards him, getting closer, as she stumbled and slipped and cursed her way along the path. She rounded a headland and below her the cliff path stretched around a bay and then up to a headland on the far side. She could see a good distance ahead of her so she stopped and studied the landscape carefully. It was now virtually light. If George was here, he would probably be stirring, if he stirred he might move, if he moved she might lose him, or spot him. She knew that once she had a fix on him, she would have to get to him quickly. She could see nothing and nothing moved. There was no colour, no bright white hair, just mile after mile of scrub, gorse and granite. She closed her eyes for a moment and concentrated hard. She felt she could see him asleep in the lea of a rock, a blanket pulled up to his chin, a brown blanket, not very helpful at all. She shook her head to clear it. Keith Penrose would not approve of such fantasies. The sensible thing was to keep walking and if George was on the coastal path then she would find him.

She was half way around the bay when slipping and sliding she ground to a halt, falling heavily onto her bottom, a carefully placed sharp stone digging into her coccyx. It was very painful. This was hopeless, her family had to be worried sick about her and this so called sixth sense of hers was doing her no good, nor more importantly, George. The path was close to the cliff edge again at this point. She scrambled unsteadily to her feet and looked over. There was a drop of at least three hundred feet, onto jagged rocks. She could so easily have fallen, but equally so could George. It was a heart-stopping moment, imagining that little body tumbling over and over. The nightmare of such a scenario strengthened her – she just had to find him.

It was virtually daylight now and soon, she imagined, there would be other searchers out on the cliff. She was starting forward when something caught her eye. It was not anything particularly bright, pale yellow in colour, easy to miss, but it looked like a strap and it was protruding from the side of a rock a few feet ahead of her and above. It looked like the strap of a rucksack.

She walked towards it as quietly as she could. During the night she had thought long and hard about how she would approach George, if she found him. What terrified her most was the thought that he might run off and if he ran off he might fall. This was a very dangerous place for an eight year old in a panic. Her heart was beating so loudly that she could hear it drumming in her ears. She walked past the rock. As close quarters the strap looked clean and new, not something discarded days, weeks or months before. She crept around the rock and carefully levered herself up … and there he was, just as she had seen him in her head. He was using his rucksack as a pillow, the brown blanket was pulled up to his chin and sticking out just above the blanket was the reassuring ear of what was obviously a much favoured teddy bear. A lump rose in her throat, tears leapt into her eyes. Poor little boy was all that she could think. He was very still and for a moment she panicked. Was he unconscious, was he even … but perhaps the scrutiny of her eyes disturbed him or the growing light, for he sighed a little and turned slightly in his sleep. She was still wondering whether and how to wake him when his eyes snapped open, big round and blue, like his sister's, she thought with a stab of misery. He looked terrified and began scrambling into a sitting position. She put her hand on his arm.

'It's alright George, I'm a friend.' Talking was what she needed to do, if she got it wrong now, she could lose him. She smiled at him. 'Not a very comfortable night, was it? I spent the night out here too, a bit further along the cliff towards St Ives. I feel very stiff this morning.'

George looked at her quizzically. 'Why did you sleep out here?'

'I was looking for you,' she said.

'Oh,' his eyes clouded.

'It's okay,' she said, 'don't worry, don't worry about anything. Everything is fine, nobody is cross.'

'I expect Granny and Gramps will be cross.'

'No, no they won't,' Felicity said. There was a moment's silence between them.

George looked at her wearily. 'Who are you,' he said, 'are you the police?'

'No.'

He stared at her. 'I saw you before in St Ives in the pasty shop.'

'That's right,' she said, 'shall I tell you a story?'

He nodded. She lowered herself onto a rock and the gesture seemed to relax him. He leaned back, settling himself to listen.

'It begins with your sister Megan.'

'She died,' he said, 'she died in a car crash. I was in the car crash but I don't remember it.'

'I know,' said Felicity. 'I know your family because I taught at St Leonard's. I taught art and I

201

taught your sister for several years.'

'I don't remember my sister, only from photos.' He suddenly looked very small and forlorn. The desire to hug him was almost overwhelming but Felicity knew it would be a grave mistake.

'I remember her,' she said, 'she was a very nice girl and very good at art.'

'Is that how you know me?' George said.

'Not exactly,' Felicity took a deep breath. 'The day of the accident I was in the school playground when your mum came to collect Megan and I saw you then. I saw you in your baby seat in the back of the car and then when I saw you again in St Ives, I recognised you.'

George seemed to accept this as being entirely logical.

'So in the pasty shop you just wanted to say hello? What's your name?'

'My name is Felicity but my friends call me Fizzy.'

'I thought you were somebody coming to take me away from Gramps, Fizzy. I sort of ran away from Dad, too, you see.'

'You've been doing rather a lot of running away by the sounds of it,' Felicity said. George nodded his head.

'My dad was on a business trip and he left me with this stinky au pair whose name is Brigitte. She always had her boyfriend round and she never gave me proper food and was always telling me to shut up and watch television, so I rang Granny and Gramps and they came and got me.'

'I spoke to the police yesterday,' Felicity said. 'Your dad will be home now, I think. He flew into Heathrow yesterday.'

'Heathrow, are you sure,' said George, 'he normally flies from Bristol?'

Felicity shrugged. 'That's what the policeman told me. Anyway, I expect Dad is on his way down here and you can ask him to get rid of that stinky au pair, I'm sure he will.' They smiled at one another. 'Why did you run away from Granny and Gramps?' Felicity asked after a moment.

'Because they were having an argument,' said George. 'They don't usually shout at one another, not like Mum and Dad used to, but yesterday they were shouting and shouting, I don't know what about I just didn't want to hear anymore of it so I decided to go away and manage on my own, only it wasn't very nice when it got dark.'

'No it wasn't, was it,' said Felicity, 'I didn't like it either and I'm supposed to be grown up.'

George's blue gaze met hers for a moment and his bottom lip trembled. 'I just wanted my mum,' he said, 'and she's dead, you know.'

'I know,' said Felicity and held out her arms to him.

They had a good hug and a good cry and it made them both feel better. When Felicity had used a none too clean handkerchief to wipe first George's grubby face and then her own, she stood up, a little shakily.

'Well,' she said, 'I think it's about time I rescued you, don't you? There is a shortcut back to Zennor across the fields. If we go back along the cliff path just a little way we'll find the path. It can't be more than a mile and a half across the fields and it's easy walking. I'm fed up of slipping and sliding over the stones aren't you?'

George nodded and took the hand she held out to pull him up.

'Have you got any food or anything to drink?' he asked. Felicity shook her head. 'Have you got a mobile phone so that I can ring Granny?' Again Felicity shook her head. 'You're an absolutely hopeless rescuer,' he said.

'I know,' she said, cheerfully.

They began to amble back across the fields. George was clearly tired and Felicity was anxious to do nothing to hassle him in case he lost confidence in her. After a while they held hands and it felt comfortable, but nonetheless she was nervous – she just wanted him safe.

They were in the middle of the last field before the village, almost home in fact, when they heard the sound of the helicopter.

'Quick, let's hide,' said George.

'I don't think we should,' said Felicity, 'I think it would be better if they saw us and then everybody would know that you are safe.'

'I suppose so,' said George. 'I had a good game yesterday hiding from the helicopter.'

'And you were very, very good at it,' said Felicity laughing. 'Nobody spotted you at all. Maybe you should join the army when you grow up.'

'I might,' said George.

The helicopter appeared over the hedge, flying low. Felicity raised an arm and waved at it. The helicopter appeared to fly past and then obviously getting a sighting of George turned back and flew towards them. Just short of them it hovered and above the sound of the engine they heard the disembodied sound of a megaphone.

'Is the boy with you George Hope?' the voice called.

It was quite impossible to shout back, the noise of the helicopter was far too great. Felicity went through a pantomime. First a thumbs up, then pointing at George and another thumbs up, then pointing at the village which they had now almost reached, trying to indicate it was the direction in which they were walking.

The helicopter continued to hover for a moment and then apparently, decision made, it took off over the village and disappeared as quickly as it had come.

'So why didn't they rescue us?' George asked, a little belligerently.

'I don't suppose they could land here, there are a lot of rocks and boulders about,' Felicity said calmly.

'They could have lowered someone on a winch to get us.' The weariness in George's voice made Felicity's heart bleed for him.

'Come on George, we can do it. Look we're only yards away now.'

They trudged along in silence for a few minutes. Felicity longed to take his hand again but sensed it would be the wrong thing to do. She was searching her mind for something to say, when George suddenly asked, 'Why do you live in Cornwall now and not in Oxford?'

'My husband died,' said Felicity, 'and I thought I needed a change, needed to do something different. It was a bit sad staying on in the house without him so I thought I'd start again.'

'Everyone dies,' George said.

'You've still got Daddy and Granny and Gramps,' Felicity said, in a brave attempt to sound cheerful.

'I don't know Dad very well,' George said in a small voice, 'I hardly ever see him.'

'Well he's a busy man, isn't he, he has a business to run.'

'But he's not interested in me, he's only interested in his business and making lots of money.'

'Would you rather live with Granny and

Gramps?' Felicity asked.

'Much rather,' said George. 'They live by this cool farm and they let me muck about and get muddy. We've only got this tiny little garden at Dad's house, we're right in the middle of the town and there is nothing to do and I hate the au pairs, I hate all of them.'

'Shall we play a guessing game?' said Felicity, desperate to distract George from the misery of his circumstances. 'Let's decide who's going to be the first person to find us. Do you think it is going to be a policeman, or Granny, or Gramps or just some random walker coming across the fields from the village?'

'Granny,' said George, firmly, 'what's the prize?'

'Five pounds if you're right,' said Felicity, recklessly. She was starting to feel slightly hysterical and very, very light headed. The sun came up suddenly turning everything apricot. 'It's going to be a beautiful day George and you're safe. We've a lot to feel thankful about.'

'Of course I'm safe,' said George. 'It's you who wouldn't have been safe with no food or water. It's just as well you found me.' She couldn't argue with him.

They were nearly at the track to the village when they saw ahead four figures hurrying towards them. One figure suddenly detached itself and started to run.

'It's Granny!' George shouted, starting to run too. Clara swept George up into a huge bear hug. Over the top of his head she looked at Felicity and smiled. 'Thank you,' she mouthed.

The other three figures materialised into Tom Gresham, Jack Curnow and Keith Penrose. While his grandparents fussed over George, Penrose did the policeman's equivalent of fussing over Felicity.

'Are you alright, Mrs Paradise?'

'Fine thank you, Inspector Penrose.'

'Good. Where did you find him?'

'Up on Zennor Tor.'

'You've been there all night, I gather.'

'How do you know that?' Felicity asked.

'I've had your daughter on to me since dawn in a right old tizz.'

'My mobile ran out of battery.'

'So I gather,' he said. 'I should be giving you a lecture about being irresponsible but I'm just so glad you've got the boy. It must have been like looking for a needle in a haystack. Certainly you succeeded where the Royal Navy and Devon and Cornwall Constabulary seemed to have singularly failed.' He looked at her quizzically for a moment and smiled. 'I suppose you were helped by one of your little moments.'

'Not exactly,' said Felicity, 'but I felt I knew where he was and well, I suppose I was right. I found him, though in fairness, George spent all yesterday hiding from you, so it's hardly surprising you didn't find him'

Tom Gresham detached himself from his wife and grandson and came over to Felicity, extending a hand. 'We've never met formally before, Mrs Paradise, but thank you so much for finding George. I don't know how you did it but I'm very grateful.' Felicity shook his hand. A nice man, she thought, she could well see why George had felt so comfortable in his company. Tom Gresham hesitated. 'It is extraordinary how you seem to become involved with our family in moments of crisis.'

'I wish that were not the case, Mr Gresham,' Felicity said with a sad smile.

'Take comfort from the fact that George could be at the bottom of a cliff, but for you.' Keith Penrose interrupted unexpectantly. Felicity gave him a grateful smile.

'Fizzy, Fizzy, you owe me five pounds,' George said, rushing up to them.

'Whatever for?' asked Clara.

'I bet Fizzy that you'd be the first person we saw Granny, and you were.'

'Is this true,' said Inspector Penrose gravely. 'Was this a formal undertaking, Mrs Paradise?'

'I'm afraid it was, inspector and to my deep embarrassment I'm afraid to say I have no money on me. I set off from home yesterday on what I thought was a short sketching expedition.'

'Well to avoid having to arrest you for fraud,' said Inspector Penrose, 'I think in the circumstances it's probably up to me to honour your debt.' He felt in his breast pocket and produced a wallet from which he extracted a crisp five pound note. 'Here you are, George,' he said, handing it over to George, 'consider the debt settled.'

'Thank you very much,' said George, looking very pleased. He eyed Felicity thoughtfully for a moment. 'She's very nice,' he said to no one in particular, 'but she is a very bad rescuer.'

An ambulance was waiting outside the Tinners' and causing quite a stir. A small group of people stood around, ghoulishly waiting to see who was to be loaded into it. Clearly, the sight of a grubby little boy and an equally grubby middle-aged woman, with no sign of blood or fractured limbs, was something of a disappointment and the crowd soon dispersed.

'What's this for?' Felicity demanded.

'I'm afraid after a night in the open, you'll both need to go to hospital in Truro for a check up,' Keith said.

'Cool,' said George, 'we didn't get to go in the helicopter, but an ambulance will be just as good if we can have a siren and flashing lights. Can we have a siren?'

A smiling paramedic helped George into the ambulance, followed by Clara. 'I should think that can be arranged, young man.'

Felicity pulled Keith aside. 'I'm not going in that,' she said firmly, 'it's a ridiculous over-reaction. Of course George should go, but I just want to go home. I am absolutely fine.'

'Mrs Paradise, it's standard procedure in these sort of circumstances,' Keith said, bravely, given the light of defiance in Felicity's eyes.

'I'm not going,whatever anyone says,' she said.

'Sir,' said Jack, materialising at his boss's side. 'What about a compromise? Maybe you could run Mrs Paradise to St Ives and drop her at Stennack Surgery. Her doctor could give her a quick check up there to save going to Truro, and I can get a lift back to the station with one of the lads.'

The practicality of his suggestion was undeniable – Felicity and Keith Penrose were united in waving George off in the ambulance, lights flashing and siren blaring, as requested.

'I've got clearance to take you to the surgery. Come on,' Penrose said, 'you must be absolutely exhausted.'

'It wasn't a very comfortable night, I have to admit.'

They drove back along the road to St Ives and at a lay-by Keith pulled the car off the road and they sat in silence for a moment.

'So what do you make of the family?' Keith asked.

'I've never met Philip Hope except in court,' said Felicity, 'and then what I saw of him I didn't like, but then in the circumstances I wouldn't have done, would I? The grandparents seem really nice people and George is obviously devoted to them. He told me he'd rather live with them than his father.'

'I'm sure he would,' said Keith. 'I certainly would in his shoes.'

'Is there anything you can do, inspector?'

'Not really, no. I could alert social services to keep an eye on him, I suppose, but even then I really have no justification for doing so. George is not being ill-treated or abused in any way. He's a well fed, well educated little boy and in the eyes of the law he belongs with his father until he reaches the age of eighteen.' They were silent for a moment. 'The other problem is,' said Keith. 'that quite apart from George's welfare the thing that I'm no nearer solving is who killed his mother and why. I know how she died and I know where she died but why she died is still a complete mystery. I have never come across a case as serious as this where I appear to be at a complete dead end.'

'The grandparents weren't able to help?' Felicity asked.

Keith shook his head. 'No, not really. In the last few months, it appears that Lizzie Hope had managed to conquer her drink problem. She wanted to get her son back or at least have access to him and she knew the only way for this to happen was to stop drinking once and for all. It seems, on the face of it, she was succeeding.'

'Then the person with the obvious motive, is Philip,' said Felicity.

'Yes,' said Keith, 'but he was in Frankfurt.'

'Maybe he wasn't,' Felicity said. 'There was one thing George said to me on the walk back when I told him his father was back home having flown into Heathrow and he said, was I sure, because his father normally flew from Bristol.'

'Well, that makes sense I suppose,' said Keith. 'From Charlbury it's probably as easy to go down to Bristol as to fight your way up the M4.'

'You're missing the point, inspector,' said Felicity.

'I normally do,' said Keith, with a heavy sigh.

'If he flew into Bristol, he would be only three hours from Truro.'

'You mean he could have interrupted his business trip to Germany to come back to Cornwall and kill his wife?'

'Something like that,' said Felicity.

'Sounds a bit far fetched to me, Mrs Paradise.'

'I agree,' she said, 'but at least it's one more theory than you had a couple of minutes ago.'

He grinned at her. 'I can't argue with that. I

don't know what I'm doing standing between you, a big hot bath and a sleep.' He smiled at her, started the engine and pulled out onto the road. 'I will check out the flights to and from Bristol though around the time of the murder.'

'Good Heavens, inspector, you're mellowing in your old age,' said Felicity.

'How do you mean?' he asked.

'It would be normally far more your style to check the Bristol flights but not to admit I could be right.'

11

The explanations and recriminations seemed to go on forever. It appeared that Mel had sat up all night and Martin with her, and while there were genuine congratulations on the finding of George, there was a fair amount of talk as to how stupid she had been, in stumbling about the cliff path in the middle of the night. Felicity was far too tired to argue. A bath was run, Martin made some excellent and much appreciated porridge and finally with a great sigh of relief she crept under her duvet and passed into a dreamless sleep.

It was nearly five o'clock by the time she woke. For a while she lay quite still, apparently unable to move. Since Charlie's death, Felicity had not really slept well and this great chunk of sleep, even though it was in the middle of the day, was a welcome interlude. She felt relaxed and extremely comfortable. A delicious smell reached her and became impossible to resist. She eased her aching body out of bed, pulled on an old pair of Charlie's pyjamas, she could not bear to throw out, and went into the kitchen. Mel was sitting at the kitchen table, apparently lost in thought.

'Hello Mum, how are you feeling?'

'Much better,' said Felicity. 'What on earth is that gorgeous smell?'

'It's shepherd's pie,' said Mel. 'I've just popped it in the oven. I thought you'd probably like a very early supper having missed lunch.'

'I am absolutely starving,' Felicity said, 'that was very thoughtful of you. Have there been any phone calls?'

'Not about the Hopes,' said Mel, 'but I have had a phone call from Josh Buchanan.'

'Really,' said Felicity, 'what did he want?'

'He's offered me a job.'

'Goodness,' said Felicity. 'And what did you say?'

'I told him to stuff it,' said Mel.

'Mel, that's not very gracious.'

'He doesn't deserve graciousness,' said Mel.

'Why ever not?'

'Oh Mum, just leave it. You're exhausted and I'm exhausted, let's have a glass of wine and an early supper.'

Felicity did as she was asked and sat at the kitchen table while Mel poured them both a glass of wine. 'Martin is coming around for supper,' Mel said with studied casualness.

'Really,' said Felicity, 'that's interesting. You two

seem to be seeing quite a lot of each other.'

'Don't start,' said Mel, 'I've had enough trouble with Annie on that subject. He is just the only person around here who is even vaguely near my age group, right.'

'I can't argue with that,' said Felicity. 'Don't break his heart though, will you Mel, he's very vulnerable.'

'What about my heart?' said Mel. 'Shouldn't you be considering mine rather than his.'

'Possibly,' Felicity agreed.

'I will admit he is very good looking. You never mentioned that when you told us all about your dramatic rescue off the boat in Newlyn. He was just Martin the coastguard, not Martin the babe.'

'Even at my advanced age, I am well aware he's good looking,' said Felicity, 'but since he's hardly in my age bracket, I suppose I didn't see it as relevant.'

Martin arrived and the three of them sat comfortably around the kitchen table with a bottle of wine, the shepherd's pie and Felicity's tales of rescuing George.

'It's good in a way. After the terrible tragedy of poor little Megan it's extraordinarily satisfying that you were able to restore George to them,' said Martin.

'The Greshams made that connection too,' said Felicity, 'but I really can't relate one to the other. I may have helped George but I still failed to help Megan.'

'Oh Mum, for heaven's sake, you can't keep slaving yourself over this,' said Mel, clearly exasperated.

'I'm not,' said Felicity, instantly defensive, 'and you're right, Martin, it does help in a kind of way. I thought about it a lot during last night when I couldn't sleep on my blessed rock. I kept thinking about what would happen when I found George, what if he ran off and fell over the cliff, what if I was responsible for both those children's deaths.'

'But you weren't,' said Martin, cheerfully. 'George is safely tucked up in the little cottage in Zennor with his grandparents.'

In fact Martin could not have been more wrong. George was sitting miserably in the back of his father's car, halfway up the A30 on his way back home. No one had tried to argue when his father had appeared angrily in the middle of the afternoon and demanded that since his grandparents were clearly unable to care for their grandson, he was to come home immediately. His grandparents didn't argue because they knew it would upset George. George didn't argue because he was just too exhausted and miserable.

'I suppose we should find it a welcome relief that Mrs Paradise isn't always right,' Inspector Penrose grumbled at Jack. He had come into work early, hoping that this was the day he would see a crack of daylight appearing in his murder case, but there was none. At the time poor Lizzie Hope was being strangled, her husband, Philip, was in a crisis meeting in Frankfurt with his major customer and his bankers. Philip had been more talkative than usual when Keith had telephoned him to ask for an alibi for the time of the murder.

'So what did you think I did, inspector, hopped on a quick plane home, murdered my wife and flew back again in time for dinner?'

'It's a routine question we ask everybody associated with a serious crime,' Keith had said, levelly. God he didn't like this man. But for George, he almost wished Philip Hope was the murderer.

'As if I didn't have enough troubles already inspector, I'm fighting for my financial future at the moment. The software packages I produce are now being made a lot cheaper in China and if my major customer decides to start buying there, I'm finished, my business will collapse like a pack of cards. That's why I had to go to Frankfurt so urgently and that is why it was difficult to extricate myself when I heard about my ex-wife's death – not that it is any of your damn business.'

'I appreciate you being so frank, sir,' Keith said, aware that the irony was completely lost on Philip.'May I have the name of one or two of the people you were with at the time because I will need to verify what you have told me.'

'That's going to do a great deal to improve my chances of keeping the business, isn't it? It's wonderful PR strategy to ask your major customer to provide an alibi to demonstrate you didn't murder your ex-wife. That will finish the chances of me keeping the contract, I imagine.'

'You never know, sir,' said Keith, 'maybe you'll get the sympathy vote.' He was rewarded by Philip slamming down the phone.

Ten minutes later Philip's secretary rang and provided Keith with two telephone numbers from which he was able to establish the time and length of the meeting, its location and confirmation that Philip had been present throughout. Just to be on the safe side – for over the years Keith had become sufficiently cynical to trust no one – he arranged for the police in Frankfurt to pay a visit on both the banker and the potentially unfaithful customer to verify their statments. Both alibis had checked out and the reports were sitting on his desk now. He handed them over to Jack who studied them in silence for a moment.

'Well, boss,' Jack said, 'I know we don't like him but I don't think he murdered his ex-wife.'

'I'm very much afraid you're right,' said Penrose, heavily.

Felicity was sitting in her favourite chair in Annie's kitchen, pulled up close to the Aga. She still felt very stiff from her ordeal and the warmth was comforting. Annie regarded her quizzically. 'So, what do you reckon to Martin and your Mel then?'

Felicity shrugged her shoulders. 'I just don't know, Annie. The trouble is I don't really feel I know Mel any more, sometimes I wonder whether I ever did. She is so brittle with me, so dismissive. I can't imagine her ever taking me into her confidence.' She looked sharply at Annie. 'Has she ever confided in you, Annie?'

'No, but I'm a little worried about a romance blossoming there. On the face of it, they might bring each other comfort but the fact is they have both suffered a great deal.'

'Suffered a great deal – Mel, do you really think so, Annie?' Felicity was both shocked and defensive.

Annie reached out a hand and patted her. 'Don't take on so, my bird, she hasn't suffered through any fault of yours but she has lost her father who she loved dearly, and also her career, to which she was completely committed. It's not as bad as what has happened to Martin of course – it was truly terrible losing his wife and baby like that – but none the less,' Annie hesitated, 'Martin has known happiness and fulfilment and in a strange kind of way it gives you a strength – you've lost it but at least you've had it. In Mel's case, other than her father, it seems she has difficultly forming close relationships – that's what I meant by 'suffered'.'

'How can you say that's not my fault?' said Felicity. 'Of course it's my fault, I'm her mother. If she has difficultly making relationships then that is down to me.'

'It really isn't,' said Annie. 'She is very competitive, your Mel. I bet that even as a tiny child she worked out a role for herself within the family. Forgive me for saying this, but I'm only repeating what you've told me – your son Jamie was something of a disappointment to his father so when Mel came along she saw there was a ready-made role for her as the apple of her daddy's eye, and she went for it. Your husband obviously encouraged her and she was a very bright child so reading law was no difficultly for her. Now, however, she has lost her hero and she's all at sea. We all make choices, my bird, even as children and we spend the rest of our life living with the consequences.'

'I should have seen it,' said Felicity, 'I should have given her a more balanced, broader childhood. I should have recognised I was neglecting her.' Felicity put her head in her hands, the silence between them lengthened.

'What makes you think you neglected her, my girl?' Annie asked gently, after a while.

Felicity hesitated, 'Let me tell you what a typical evening was like at home and judge for yourself.'

'Go on then,' said Annie, she stood up and put

the kettle back on the Aga.

'Well, when the children would came back from school, we always liked to eat as a family. As Charlie was a partner by the time the children reached school age, he could usually be home in good time. They would come in, have juice and biscuits and then go off and do their prep before supper.'

'Right,' said Annie.

'In the case of Mel, she simply went upstairs, did her prep, came down and usually had half an hour or so before supper to mess about. If her father was home, she would go and see him. In the winter they would play cards or chess, in the summer they would go round to the Parks sometimes and play tennis or chuck a ball about.'

'So what was Jamie doing while all this was going on?' Annie asked.

'Struggling with his prep, of course,' said Felicity. 'I would be cooking supper, he'd have his prep at the kitchen table and he'd struggle and struggle.'

'Did Charlie ever come and help?'

'Very occasionally but he used to become irritated very quickly because Jamie was very much in awe of his father and so would go to pieces when Charlie started asking him questions. Charlie wasn't very tactful, he'd say things that were hurtful without meaning to, and that made everything worse, of course. The other problem was that if

Charlie came and joined in to help Jamie, Mel did too. Although Mel is two years younger than Jamie, she could always do his prep with her eyes closed and one hand tied behind her back. So, on the whole I didn't encourage it, they undermined Jamie and made him worse. He was much better on his own with me.'

'So did Jamie have learning difficulties?' Annie asked.

'No, not really, he was just slower than Mel, you couldn't say he was dyslexic or had any specific problem.'

'Boys often are slower than girls,' Annie said.

'In Jamie's case, he was an IT boffin but of course we didn't know, not until he had his first computer and then that was it, he was off and everything was fine so long as he could sit in front of it. Even that used to drive Charlie mad, though. He said Jamie should be out playing sport instead of bashing the keyboard all day.'

'So your family were split into two, really.'

'That's right.'

'Has Mel ever talked to Jamie about her problems?'

'No, they're not close. Mel doesn't like Jamie's wife. It's very sad because she hardly ever sees her nephews but there is nothing I can do about it. I try bringing them together when I can but it's without a great deal of enthusiasm on either side.'

'Friends we choose, family we have thrust upon us,' said Annie, sagely.

'I just feel so hopelessly inadequate,' said Felicity after a moment, accepting gratefully the cup of tea Annie placed in front of her. 'If Charlie was alive he would have got hold of Michael Ferguson and given him hell and wanted to know exactly why Mel hadn't been taken on and then he'd have found her new chambers, built up her confidence, sorted the whole thing out.'

'I don't know why I am saying this exactly,' said Annie, 'but if Charlie was alive Mel wouldn't have lost her job.'

'Really,' said Felicity, 'what on earth makes you think that?'

Annie shrugged her shoulders again. 'I've absolutely no idea, just a feeling and I tell you what else I feel.'

'What's that?' Felicity asked.

'I think it's about time you two started talking to one another instead of talking through me.'

'I'm sorry, Annie, you're right, of course.'

'It's okay, my pet, it's just that the story you've just told me, Mel has told me too, more or less. You both mind the fact that you can't communicate, mind it dreadfully, you both care deeply for one another and it's about time you started telling each other so.'

On the way back from Annie's, Felicity popped into Chris Bailey's chandlery shop. The shop was empty and Chris was scooping large quantities of cream out of a tub and smearing it on his hands, which looked red raw and very sore.

'What's wrong Chris, you haven't been beating up your customers again, have you?'

'No,' he said, smiling. 'I have infective dermatitis, it's caused by the nickel in my brasses. A chandlery is absolutely the wrong business for my skin, all these ships bells, barometers and the like, they play havoc on my hands, especially when I clean them.'

Felicity stared at his poor hands. 'They certainly look very uncomfortable.'

'I hear you had a bit of a run in on the cliff. You did well to find the boy. Have you seen the Greshams since? Chris asked.

'No,' said Felicity, surprised. 'I didn't know you knew them, Chris.'

'I've known the family for years, since the little girl, Megan was a baby. They used to own a cottage, down Back Road East, close to Porthmeor beach, it were.' Chris began rubbing the cream into his hands.

'I wish I'd known, I could have asked you about George weeks ago – all along you would have been able to tell me who he really was. How infuriating,'

'I certainly know George – the boy's had to go home with his father now.'

'Already, but when did he go?' Felicity was appalled.

'Yesterday afternoon.'

'But that was the day I found him. He must have been exhausted – poor child.'

'Philip was in a right temper, apparently, the Greshams didn't know what to do because they didn't want any more rows in front of George. As soon as the boy was discharged from hospital, Philip was off with him.'

'How awful – how do you know all this, Chris?'

'It's all round the town. I heard about it in the Sloop.'

'Yes, of course.'

'I don't know much about kids but if that Philip can't lighten up a bit, he's going to turn the boy into a right head case.'

Felicity thought about Chris's words as she walked home to Jericho Cottage. The awesome responsibility of parents for children. However much one cared one could still get it so horribly wrong. It was odd, Chris's interest in George and apparent concern for the Greshams. Something didn't feel quite right about it, though what, Felicity couldn't work out. For some reason, though, it left her uneasy.

Mel and Martin came home in good spirits that evening. 'We had a great day,' said Martin.

'What have you been doing?' Felicity asked.

'Trying to find Martin a market garden.'

'Really,' Felicity was interested. She poured three glasses of wine; supper was in the oven. It was hard not to warm to the two of them, they looked so happy and relaxed compared to how she had seen each of them at various times. She put firmly to the back of her mind Annie's words about two damaged people. 'So what's this all about, Martin?'

'Well,' said Martin. 'It's silly to put all my money into a house at the moment. I don't really feel much like setting up a serious home on my own, I'm not really ready for that. But I am ready for work and rather than go back to working for someone, I thought maybe I could start my own business.'

'That sounds a brilliant idea,' said Felicity, 'doing what?'

'He's got this idea about specialising in sub-tropical and exotic plants. What do you think, Mum?'

'Sounds good to me,' said Felicity.

'And also plants that grow particularly well by the coast, in other words, speciality plants,' said Martin, clearly enthused.

'We've been looking for somewhere where he can both grow them and sell them,' said Mel, 'and I think we've found it, haven't we, Martin?'

'I think so,' Martin agreed.

'Whereabouts?' Felicity asked.

'The other side of Hayle. You go down this track,' said Martin, 'and there are some semi-derelict greenhouses and a few polytunnel arcs – it used to be a daffodil farm once.'

'It sounds a bit off the beaten track,' said Felicity.

'It's not really,' said Martin, 'it's on the main Hayle to Helston road. It's just a short way down a little lane. It used to be open to the public when it was selling daffodils.'

'And what ... you can buy it?'

'Yes, I can just about afford it and then I can just rent a flat or cottage in Hayle until I can afford to buy something.'

'Annie is going to be devastated if you move out of St Ives,' said Felicity.

'Well Hayle is not exactly very far away, is it?' said Martin.

'It might as well be on the moon as far as Annie is concerned,' said Felicity, affectionately, 'but I'm very pleased for you. What's the place called?'

'It's called Morgan's Farm,' Martin said. 'Someone suggested Martin's Farm but I won't change the name, it's bad luck.'

'Well fingers crossed you get it. Have you put in an offer?'

'Yes,' he said, 'I'll hear from the agent in the morning.'

'Well, here's to Morgan's Farm,' said Felicity

and they all raised their glasses.

Supper was friendly and easy. Felicity, still very tired from the previous day and agitated by her conversations with both Annie and Chris, drank rather more wine than usual. It was when they were sitting over coffee that she suddenly said, 'Well it looks like we've sorted out Martin's life, so what's happening in yours, Mel?' It was the wine talking and she regretted her words immediately. She knew any enquiry into the future was a red rag to a bull to Mel.

Mel's reaction was unfortunately predictable. 'Oh Mum, for heaven's sake, give it a rest.'

Martin set down his coffee mug. 'Mel, that's no way to speak to your mother.'

'Don't you start lecturing me, as well,' said Mel.

'I'm not going to sit here and listen to you being rude to a very dear friend.' He stood up. 'You need to stop treating your mother like the enemy. I've always found her very easy to talk to and it's about time you started doing the same. Just tell her what you told me this afternoon.' Without another word, he simply walked out of the door leaving mother and daughter alone and in silence, staring at one another, shocked.

'Tell me what?' Felicity asked, recovering first.

Mel shook her head. 'It doesn't matter.'

Felicity leaned forward her voice urgent. 'Mel, it does matter, Martin is right I'm not an ogre, I'm your mother and I love you. Whatever is going on in your life, please share it with me, please, I beg you, I

230

can't do more than that.'

Mel slowly raised her head and met her mother's eyes. 'I know about Dad's bribe,' she said in a very small voice that made her sound more like ten than twenty four.

Felicity felt like someone had hit her across the face. 'You know what?' she said.

'Mum don't embarrass me or yourself by pretending you don't know what I mean.'

'I wasn't going to,' said Felicity. 'I'm just wondering how on earth you know?'

Suddenly the whole story was tumbled out very easily and quickly. The row with Michael Ferguson when she tried to terminate their affair and how, unwittingly, she had cited her father as the perfect example of how to conduct oneself if one was privileged enough to practice law.

'He called me pompous, Mum, and affected, and then he said if I used my bloody father as my role model, I'd soon be in trouble. I asked him what he meant and he said that Dad had taken bribes when he was a young man. He said it was common knowledge and that Dad had been forced to leave his London law practice and start again in Oxford. "Full scale corruption is a rather more serious offence, I think you would agree, than a little sexual comfort between colleagues," was how he put it, Mum.'

'The bastard,' said Felicity, 'so what happened next?'

'I threw a book of law notes at him,' said Mel, with a trace of a smile, she seemed remarkably composed.

'Did it hurt him?' Felicity asked.

'Yes, I think so but I didn't hang around to find out. I cleared my desk and went.'

'And what made you think he's telling the truth?' Felicity asked, playing for time while her mind raced ahead of itself.

'Mum, I've worked for Michael Ferguson long enough to know he would never make up something as serious as this.'

'He's not above reproach though, is he?' Felicity said, 'presumably he lied to his wife about you?'

'That's different,' said Mel. 'I just know he was telling the truth. He was, wasn't he, Mum?'

The silence between them was very tense. Finally unable to meet her daughter's eye, Felicity simply nodded. She heard Mel catch her breath and looked up to see great tears flowing down her face.

'I'm sorry darling,' she said. 'I know how much you loved your father. I would have given anything to protect you from this.'

Mel allowed herself to be hugged and after a few minutes, once more in control, she drew away from her mother. 'Why, why did he do it?' she asked.

'He was very young and very broke and he'd had a difficult childhood – having to live two different lives.'

'How do you mean?' Mel frowned and in doing so suddenly looked heartbreakingly like her father.

'He had a very traditional and privileged education, Eton and Oxford, as you know, but he hardly had two pennies to rub together. He got to Eton on a scholarship, or rather a partial scholarship. His father had died penniless, his mother struggled to pay the bills; it was all very hard. He adored his mother. You remember Granny, don't you? She lived with us until she died when you were nearly three.' Mel nodded. 'She was a lovely woman and very different from Charlie who, I imagine, took after his father. She was such a gentle soul and devoted to her son,' Felicity hesitated and took a deep breath. 'I don't know the details, Mel and we never will now, but he went out to South Africa where he met someone who had been a friend of his father's. This person offered your father a bribe to suppress some information about his company, it's the money he used to buy Norham Gardens, and give his mother the stability she needed.'

'Our home!' Mel said. 'How awful.'

'I know how you feel,' said Felicity, 'it's why I sold it.'

'And who was this person?' Mel asked after a moment.

'It was the father of the man who was responsible, ultimately, for Dad's death.'

'Ralph Smithson's father?'

Felicity nodded.

'And you knew about this all through the years?'

'No,' said Felicity. 'I only learnt about it after Ralph Smithson had been caught. What is extraordinary is that Michael Ferguson knew.'

'I think you'll find it isn't,' said Mel, her voice suddenly hard. 'Tell me, Mum, who is the one other person who knows this story apart from you and me.'

'Josh,' said Felicity.

'I thought so and would it surprise you to know that Josh is a great friend of Michael Ferguson's brother.'

'I knew but I can't believe it Mel, I can't believe he told Michael Ferguson.'

'Well how else do you think he knows? Who else could have possibly told him? You didn't tell him, so it has to be Josh.'

'Presumably,' said Felicity, 'it's why you told Josh to stuff his job.'

'Precisely,' said Mel.

'The rat, I just can't believe it, he is supposed to have been such a friend of this family.'

'And he's my godfather, for heaven's sake.'

'There has always been something not quite right about Josh,' Felicity said thoughtfully. 'Dad never rated him, you know. He liked him, was fond of him as a chum, but always had his doubts about his integrity.'

'Dad was a fine person to be critical of anyone's

integrity,' Mel said, her voice steely.

'No, no Mel, you mustn't go down that road. I am absolutely certain that from the day your father joined the Oxford practice, his behaviour was exemplary. I'm absolutely certain of that.'

'Mum, you've no idea,' Mel said, 'it's just what you want to think.'

'It's not,' said Felicity, close to tears herself now. 'I just know Mel. He was essentially a good man. He made one mistake and he paid for it with his life.'

'Why,' said Mel, 'I don't understand, what do you mean?'

'Ralph Smithson had been trying to blackmail your father for years. Finally, when Dad refused to co-operate, Ralph had him killed.' Felicity's voice was bleak.

'Blackmailing him about what?' Mel said.

'About the fact that he had acted corruptly in accepting money from his father.'

'Oh God,' said Mel, 'what a mess.'

'It is,' said Felicity. 'and I'm going to add to it by killing Josh Buchanan.'

'No need,' said Mel, 'I'll do it for you.'

Felicity managed a small smile. 'That's what I'm slightly afraid of!'

They talked on and on; Felicity was desperate to try and keep Mel's image of her father intact. 'Dad wouldn't have wanted you to be affected by this. That would mean that the thing he did wrong, didn't die with him. He couldn't bear that.'

Mel looked at her mother, her face haunted. 'Well I'm sorry he couldn't bear that,' said Mel, 'but neither can I. I've built my life around trying to be like my father and now I find that my father isn't the sort of person I thought he was, nor the sort of person I want to be.'

'I went through that stage,' said Felicity. 'I couldn't bear the fact he hadn't confided in me when he was being threatened. I couldn't believe that he was keeping that to himself and not sharing it with me, I was so hurt.'

Mel nodded. 'Yes, I can see that.'

'But then I remembered the rest of it – his kindness, his good fun, his championing of the underdog. He was a good man Mel, he really was.'

'If you say so,' said Mel, 'but no longer the sort of person to inspire one to build a career in law.'

'Has it had that affect on you?' Felicity asked, genuinely surprised. 'Knowing you, knowing what a trouper you are, I would have thought it might have had the opposite affect. Right my father didn't get things right, so I'm jolly well going to make sure I do.'

'I agree, fighting talk is usually my style,' said Mel, 'but I don't seem to have much fight in me at the moment.'

'You're not saying you're thinking of another career altogether?'

'To be honest, Mum, I don't know what I'm thinking at the moment.'

Felicity took a coffee out onto the balcony after Mel had gone to bed. The town looked beautiful. There was a high tide and the lights reflected on the water, the fishing boats bobbing up and down. It was quite chilly but very still, even the seagulls seemed more subdued than normal. There was a tranquillity about the scene which was just what Felicity needed.

'Oh Charlie,' she said, aloud, 'talk about the sins of the father.'

It had been a difficult evening and yet, despite it, Felicity felt a small ray of hope. She and Mel had talked properly for the first time in years, if ever. They had a long way to go but it was a start, and above all, there were no more secrets.

12

Clara Gresham sat forlornly and alone in the morning room of Juniper Farmhouse. It was a cold blustery day and she knew she should be taking out the labradors for their morning constitutional but somehow she couldn't summon up the energy. On her desk there was a photograph. She looked at it every day, several times a day. It hurt to do so like having a knife thrust into the heart, but it was a necessary pain. It showed Lizzie sitting in an armchair with newborn George cradled on her lap and Megan, sitting on the arm of the chair, with her arm around her mother. They all looked very cosy and content. Megan had adored her little brother and never once shown any resentment and from the way she was looking at him in the photograph, it was clearly love at first sight. If only she had lived, for her sake of course, but for the difference it would have made to George and Lizzie too. Poor little boy, the memory of his forlorn face as Philip had driven him off from Zennor broke her heart. She knew she had to do something to help George, the question was if she wasn't very careful she could make things a great deal worse. What to do, what could she do?

The phone interrupted her thoughts and before she could summon the energy to get to it, the answer phone kicked in.

'Clara, it's Philip,' the voice said, 'come and collect George right away. He's yours now. Take care of him. Goodbye.'

Clara frowned in astonishment. She turned off the machine, rewound it and played it again. Philip's voice sounded strange, almost hysterical. She picked up the telephone and dialled 1471 – the number he had been calling from was his workplace. She rang the number but there was no reply; the phone simply rang and rang. She looked at her watch. That in itself was odd. It was five past nine. There should be somebody there, by now, besides Philip. She telephoned George's school and spoke to the school secretary. Could she check please that George had been delivered safely to school – the woman was back to her in moments. 'Yes, George was in his classroom.'

'Right,' said Clara. 'Tell George that his grandfather and I are coming to pick him up at the end of the school day so not to catch the bus.'

'He'll be very pleased about that,' said the school secretary, pleasantly.

Tom Gresham was in the yard pretending to

mend the hinges on the stable door but in fact worrying about his grandson. When he saw his wife running across the driveway towards him, he knew something was up. His heart did a flip. There had been so many dramas to cope with, he didn't know if he could bear any more. He dropped his tools and met her half way across the yard.

'What is it, what's happened?' he asked, a tremor in his voice.

'Philip wants us to collect George.'

'Why, I didn't think he ever wanted us to see George ever again, didn't trust us with his care?' Tom's voice could not disguise the bitterness he felt.

'Tom, come and listen to the answerphone message, it's most peculiar.'

Two and a half hours later, the Greshams drove into Charlbury and parked outside Mulberry House. They rang on the bell several times but there was no reply.

'We can't just collect George from school without any of his stuff,' Clara said.

'We could easily,' said Tom 'He doesn't need much, just a few clothes, a pair of trainers and a box of Lego would do it.'

They both smiled at one another. 'There's Teddy,' said Clara.

'That's true,' Tom agreed.

They stood dithering on the doorstep and tried

again. The bell echoed through the house, there was clearly no one in. Suddenly they heard someone calling. A pleasant looking woman in her early thirties, a baby on her hip, was waving to them from next door.

'Are you the Greshams'?' she called.

'Yes,' said Clara.

'Sorry, I didn't hear you drive up. This one decided to present me with the most appalling nappy. I've got the keys for you.' She disappeared inside the house and came back again holding out a bunch of keys. 'Philip asked me to give you these when you arrived.'

'What does he want me to do with them when we've finished?' Clara asked.

'He didn't say,' she said. 'You can give them back to me, if you like. My name is Jane, incidentally and this appallingly smelly person is called Jessie.'

Jessie managed a toothy grin.

'We won't be long,' said Clara. 'We're just picking up a few things for George who is coming to stay with us.'

'How lovely for you,' said Jane. 'See you later.'

As always Mulberry House was impressively tidy. The Greshams went up to George's room and packed a small bag which they found in his wardrobe with a few clothes and, of course, Teddy.

'I'm going to try ringing Philip at work again,'

Tom said, 'while you do the packing. After the last incident, we need to be careful. The police might really do us for kidnapping if we just take George again.'

'Any luck?' Clara called a few minutes later as she came down the stairs with George's belongings.

Tom was standing in the hall holding the telephone to his ear.

'Absolutely nothing.' He replaced it thoughtfully and looked at his wife. 'You know, I don't think we can just simply follow Philip's instructions, take George and go. There has to be more to this, I don't like it.'

'It sounded as though Philip wanted us to look after him forever.'

'I know, but why, particularly having taken him away from us only a couple of days ago and why is there no reply from his works? I think we should go round there.'

Clara looked at her watch. 'I suppose we've time to go out to Chipping before meeting George, but I don't know what you're trying to achieve Tom. Shouldn't we just be grateful and keep quiet?'

'George has had enough chopping and changing in his life. If, for whatever reason, Philip has decided he should come to us, then we need to be able to tell George. Also there are decisions to make – whether we should move to Oxford so that he can stay at his existing school or whether he should have a clean break and start at a school in Bath. He needs stability in his life, Clara, he needs certainty. We can't just take him in response to an answerphone message. We need to know what's going on.'

'You're right, of course,' Clara said, coming close to her husband and slipping her arm around his waist. Tom pulled her to him and she rested her head on his shoulder. 'It's just I'm so frightened that Philip will change his mind. George needs to be with us, he wants to be with us and we want him. He has no life here in this horrible cold house, his father never here and an endless stream of au pairs to look after him. I just can't bear it any more.'

'I can't either,' said Tom, 'but we can't give George any more false hopes. Come on, let's stop talking about it and go. There are still three hours before we have to pick George up from school. That's plenty of time to have this out with Philip.'

The first thing they noticed when they drove into the car park of Hope Communications was that there was only one car – Philip's.

'That's odd,' said Tom. 'Where is everybody?'

'Maybe he's given them all a holiday,' Clara suggested, 'though that's hardly his style, I would have thought.'

They parked in a visitor's space and went up to the front door. It was not locked but inside the reception was deserted.

'Is anybody around?' Tom shouted. His voice echoed back to them, the place was clearly empty.

Tom and Clara stared at one another. 'This is really creepy,' said Clara. 'How many people does he employ, thirty, forty?'

'Nearer forty, I would have said,' said Tom.

'I don't like it, Tom,' Clara said, her voice tremulous. 'Something's terribly wrong, can't you feel it? Something bad has happened here, maybe we should call the police.'

'Calm down, old girl,' Tom said, sounding much more confident than he felt. 'Philip has to be here, because his car is in the car park. Let's try and find his office.'

They didn't need to find Philip's office. As they left reception and headed towards the staircase, they saw him. He was hanging in the stairwell, the rope holding him was attached to the banister rail two floors above. Even from where they stood they could see from the angle of his neck that Philip Hope was quite dead.

'He's hanged himself,' Penrose said gloomily to Jack.

'Who has?' Jack asked.

'Philip Hope.'

'You're joking.'

'I'm not joking,' said Inspector Penrose. 'I've

just had a call from Thames Valley.'

'Then he must be guilty. Case solved, sir and that poor little boy can go and live with his grandparents – perfect solution, case dismissed.'

'Oh, that it was that easy, Jack. He's not guilty, he didn't kill his wife.'

'Then why did he top himself?'

'Money,' said Penrose, with a heavy sigh.

'Money's not worth killing yourself for,' Jack said.

'That's all very well for you and I to say,' said Penrose, 'because we don't have any. I think you'll find that people who have made a lot and then are faced with losing it, have a completely different view as to its importance.'

'Maybe, sir.'

'Anyway,' said Penrose, 'that's the view of Thames Valley. Apparently the Official Receiver had been called in to wind up Philip Hope's company. He laid off all his staff, telephoned his in-laws to come and collect George and then hanged himself.'

'Still seems a bit of an over-reaction to me, sir .'

Keith rose to his feet. 'And it still doesn't solve our murder.'

'Are you going out sir ?'

'Yes.'

'Do you want me to drive you?'

'No thank you,' said Penrose.

'Can I ask where you are going, sir ?'

'I'm going to see Mrs Paradise,' Keith stopped at the door. 'I think I should tell her personally about Philip Hope – she's so emotionally entangled with that family. In any event, she's a good person to talk to when facing a brick wall.'

'What shall I do, sir ?'

'Find a motive and a murderer, young Curnow, or we're both going to be back directing traffic.'

Her reaction to his news was very predictable. She sat down carefully at the kitchen table. 'George,' she said, 'where is George, is he alright?'

'He is back with his grandparents, in Bath, at their home.'

Felicity nodded. She smiled the ghost of a smile. 'I don't think either of us could go through the 'where's George' scenario again, inspector, do you?' He shook his head. 'It was kind of you to come and tell me.'

'I thought I would come in person. I know how involved you are with the family. I didn't want you to hear it on the news or even have me tell you about it over the phone.'

'Would you like a drink – coffee, glass of wine?'

'No, nothing thanks, Mrs Paradise.'

'You don't feel like a walk, do you?' said Felicity. 'I feel a bit agitated, I think I need to move about.'

'I'd love a walk,' said Keith. 'I think agitated is

what I feel, too.'

They set off for the Island, via Porthmear beach. The tide was in and the sea rough so they did not talk until they climbed up the steps on to the Island itself. They walked along to the bench which overlooked the beach and, without discussing it, sat down and stared out to sea.

'So I presume this means he killed Lizzie?' Felicity said after a lengthy pause.

'No, quite the contrary,' said Keith, 'his alibi checked out, it's absolutely bullet-proof. This is nothing to do with Lizzie and nor, before you start trying to blame yourself, is it anything to do with Megan. It is about his business, it's gone bust, and he couldn't take it.'

'If he'd had a wife and a daughter as well as a son he'd probably have survived,' Felicity said in a small voice.

'You can twist things around and blame yourself for pretty much everything, if you want to,' Keith said, 'but in this case, Mrs Paradise, you'd be wrong. I know it's not good to speak ill of the dead but Philip Hope wasn't a very nice man. He was obsessed with his business and his status within the industry and presumably money mattered a great deal. By all accounts he wasn't a good father to George nor, if Mr and Mrs Gresham are to be believed, was he a good husband either. Think of the selfishness of taking George away from his grandparents in Zennor when he must have already been at least contemplating suicide. One doesn't wish him dead nor the anguish of mind necessary to even contemplate suicide, but the buck stops with him – there is no one else to blame.'

'Well, that's your opinion,' said Felicity.

'My mother was a very wise woman,' Penrose said after a moment. 'She had a little saying which was that – 'guilt is nothing more than self indulgence'.'

'I need to think about that one,' said Felicity.

'Her philosophy was that if something had happened and you felt that you were to blame, sitting around beating your breast about it was not going to make anything better. The way ahead was to put it right, if you could, and if you couldn't, move on.'

'Easier to say if you're not talking about the death of a child,' Felicity said staring out to sea.

'Mrs Paradise, I'm going to say this once more and once more only. Lizzie Hope killed her daughter. She was a consenting adult who drank too much and very irresponsibly drove her children when she was in no fit state to do so. That is the beginning, middle and end of what happened to poor little Megan Hope.'

Felicity turned to him and smiled. 'You are a very nice man, Inspector Penrose.'

'I don't think most of my colleagues would agree

with you at the moment.'

'Why?' Felicity asked.

'I'm like a bear with a sore head – the combination of Carly and then getting absolutely nowhere with this murder. I know I'm not the easiest person to work with at the moment.'

'How is Carly?'

'Better, she is going for a check-up next week. She has stopped being sick but she has awful night sweats so that means she doesn't sleep very well – nonetheless she manages to be cheerful, amazingly cheerful.' They lapsed into silence. 'I love watching the surfers,' Keith said after a moment, nodding towards the beach, 'so clever those kids and so nice to see them doing something other than hang around street corners smoking spliffs.'

'You're sounding a bit like a grumpy old man,' Felicity said, smiling.

'I take it, Mrs Paradise, that insulting a police officer, in this instance, is an indication that you're cheering up a little.'

She smiled back. 'So if Philip Hope didn't murder Lizzie, who did, inspector?'

'I don't know,' said Penrose with a deep sigh. 'That's my problem. I am completely and utterly stuck. The thought did cross my mind that if Philip didn't kill her maybe Tom Gresham did.'

'What can you be saying inspector, that Tom Gresham killed his own daughter?'

'He loves that boy very much, he'd do anything to protect him. His daughter was a drunk, had been responsible for the death of his granddaughter, maybe she was making demands or …' his voice trailed away. Felicity shook her head at him in disbelief. 'He was in the army,' Keith continued, 'a successful soldier, a brigadier by the time he retired, a man of action, it's not impossible,' he finished, lamely.

'Inspector, you are a man of action. Is there anything in the world that Carly could do or say that would make it possible for you to murder her?'

'No, of course not,' said Keith, genuinely shocked.

'Well then, think about it, you like the Greshams, don't you?' Keith nodded. 'I do too. They're normal, nice people to whom terrible, abnormal things have happened but that wouldn't have turned Tom Gresham into a killer, would it, anymore than it would turn you into one?'

Keith shook his head. 'Can we walk again?' he said.

They stood up and began walking around the Island. As they turned the corner and caught sight of Godrevy lighthouse, the wind hit them. They walked on in silence and climbed the steep steps by the coastguard's look out. At the top, sheltered by the wind again, they stopped and gazed out across St Ives.

'Philip didn't do it, Tom didn't do it, so who on

earth did?' Keith said almost to himself. 'I'm missing something, I'm getting too old for this game, the brain doesn't work like it used to. We know, or think we know, that Lizzie got off the train at Truro because of where her body was found, but we don't know what time she left Oxford, and no one, no one, Mrs Paradise, remembers her at Truro station, being picked up or getting a taxi. No one remembers her on the train – including, mark you, the ticket inspector – the great British public seem to have been walking around that day with their eyes closed. I am in despair.'

'Oh come on, inspector, stop feeling sorry for yourself. You've just given me a lecture about self indulgence. I'd have thought feeling sorry for yourself was far more self indulgent than feeling guilty.'

Keith turned and grinned at her. 'You're right, of course.' He pointed down to Porth Gwidden car park. 'Surely it's Martin Trethewey getting into that battered old car of his?'

'Yes, it is,' said Felicity, shielding her eyes.

'And who is that gorgeous blonde with him? Life must be improving for him by the look of things, lucky devil.'

'That gorgeous blonde is my daughter,' said Felicity, evenly.

'Really, I am so sorry, that sounded awful. How rude of me.' Keith was mortified.

'You weren't rude, inspector, it's fine.'

'Are they an 'item'?' he asked. 'At least I think that's the word?'

'No, I don't think so,' said Felicity, 'although I'm not entirely sure.'

'Would you approve if they were?'

Felicity smiled. 'Is any man ever going to be good enough for Carly, inspector?'

Keith smiled back. 'No, of course not.'

'Then you have my answer. Would you like to come and meet her?'

'I don't think so, not just at the moment, I don't feel very sociable. I hope you understand.'

'I understand completely,' said Felicity. 'I don't feel very sociable either. I keep thinking about poor little George and how they are going to tell him about his father's death and what he's going to think. Oh, life can be so cruel sometimes.'

They started down the hill and suddenly Felicity stopped short. 'Inspector has it ever occurred to you that perhaps Philip Hope isn't George's father?'

'No,' said Keith. 'I can't say it ever has. What would make you say such a thing, Mrs Paradise?'

'Only that there was quite a gap in age between George and Megan. Megan was eight when George was born. It seems a bit odd.'

'I don't suppose all that drink made it easy for Lizzie to conceive and the drinking probably wouldn't have made them the best of friends, husband and wife, if you see what I mean.' Keith suggested.

'Yes, I see what you mean,' said Felicity, 'but it is a theory you might like to explore. Philip seems never to have taken to his son, when in the circumstances, you'd think he'd be moving heaven and earth to make it up to the boy for what he'd lost.'

'I did ask Mrs Gresham about a boyfriend, apparently there was no one in Lizzie's life.'

'Not now, not recently,' said Felicity, 'but perhaps there was some years ago, when she was still drinking.'

Inspector Penrose shook his head. 'I can't see it.'

'Okay, okay,' said Felicity, 'you come up with a better idea then, or any idea at all, come to that.'

They both laughed. 'You're the witch,' he said. 'You're the one who is supposed to solve my cases for me – you and your sixth sense.'

'I found you George,' said Felicity. 'I think I've shot my bolt with this one, I think it's all down to you now, inspector.'

13

It was hard to tell how George was taking the news. He had cried when they had first told him.

Thames Valley Police had been very good about letting them leave as soon as they had formally identified the body so that they could collect George. None-the-less, they had been late arriving at the school, having telephoned ahead. George was in the secretary's office, doing his prep. He was very pleased to see them but clearly puzzled.

They had discussed it in the car as they had driven over to Oxford, hardly able to take in this new disaster which had struck their family. Any way they looked at it, they could see no justification for not telling George of his father's death straight away. If they kept it from him during the long journey back to Grittleton and tried to make false jolly conversation, it would be hideous, and when they did eventually tell him, George would want to know why they hadn't told him straight away. In any event he was bound to ask why he was coming to stay with them and they couldn't lie to him.

They sat him in the car, Clara in the back with him, Tom in the front turning round to face them both. It was Tom who had broken the news. He spared no details, he told George exactly what had happened and why he believed his father had killed himself.

'Did you see Daddy this morning?' Clara asked, gently. George nodded. 'Did he seem okay?'

George nodded again. 'He asked me if I loved you and Gramps?'

'And what did you say?' Tom asked.

'I said yes, of course,' said George, 'and he said good, that was all and then he went to work. Brigitte gave me breakfast and then I went to school. The Coopers down the road did the school run. Daddy does the school run sometimes but they took me this morning. Is he really dead?'

Clara put an arm around him. 'Yes George, I'm afraid he is.'

It was then that George had cried. Tom had started to drive home, Clara had held the small body to her and after a while the tears had stopped and he had slept.

Now he was tucked up in bed, Tom was taking a shower and Clara was sitting alone in the morning room again, where she had been this morning when they had received Philip's call. What a long time ago that seemed.

What to do, that was the thing, what to do

now? She longed to tell Tom the whole story, she longed to tell the police the whole story but how could she? She didn't dare, for it might mean losing George again.

'Martin has asked me to join him in his market garden venture,' Mel said, regarding her mother carefully from under her fringe. They were having lunch at the Seafood Café having not really seen one another since their big talk about Charlie.

'So what did you tell him?' Felicity asked, trying to keep her mind and thoughts very neutral. Mothers aren't allowed opinions, she reminded herself.

'It's very tempting,' said Mel, 'but I said no.'

'I hope you said it nicely and kindly.'

'Oh, Mum, for heaven's sake, of course I said it nicely and kindly, as you put it, only there doesn't seem much point in having spent all those years slogging away in the study of the legal system to end up potting plants and heaving sacks of compost about.'

'It's an honourable profession, a gardener,' Felicity said.

'You don't really think I should take him up on his offer, do you?'

Felicity smiled. 'No I don't, darling, I really don't, but I'm frightened to be too definite about anything in case I get my head bitten off.'

'As if I would,' Mel said, grinning too.

'And have you noticed,' said Felicity, 'I haven't immediately asked what you are going to do instead. You must be finally training me.'

'So you're not interested in what I'm going to do instead?' Mel said.

'Absolutely not,' said Felicity, firmly.

'So I'll just have to tell you any way,' said Mel, with a theatrical sigh. 'I'm going to apply to a law firm, but I'm going to change direction. I've decided I'd like to practise family law and I thought I'd like to do it here in the West Country.'

'Oh Mel,' said Felicity, 'that's wonderful.' She grasped her daughter's hand and squeezed it.

'Don't get too excited. I'll probably end up in Exeter initially because I should start with a relatively large firm. Once qualified, though, I could move further west. I'm going to stop being pathetic and ring Michael Ferguson tomorrow and get him to point me in the right direction. He owes me that.'

'He most certainly does,' said Felicity, 'the rat. What made you choose the West Country, I'm obviously thrilled to bits but I thought you'd go back to London?'

'Someone has to keep on eye on you,' said Mel, 'someone has to stop you wandering about on the edge of cliffs in the middle of the night.'

'And it's nothing to do with you and Martin?'

'You never give up, do you, Mum? There isn't a me and Martin at the moment, we're just friends.'

'But could there be?' Felicity persisted.

'Possibly,' Mel conceded.

'He's quite a lot older than you,' Felicity ventured.

'His wife was my age when she died,' Mel said. 'I know it was awful for you when Dad died, Mum, but for Martin to lose his wife when she was pregnant, it must have been so terrible.'

'I know, I know,' said Felicity, 'in those early days when I first came to St Ives, after Dad died, I used to think if Martin is coping, I have no excuse not to. I'm pleased you have him for a friend if nothing else.'

'He is very attractive,' said Mel. 'I recognise I do have to make my mind up about him soon, otherwise someone else will snap him up.' Felicity thought it was prudent to say nothing.

'Actually I had a specific reason for asking you out for lunch today,' she said. 'I was wondering what you thought we should do about James?'

'In what respect?' said Mel.

'Whether we should tell him about Dad and the bribe.'

'What do you think?' Mel countered.

'I'm going up to Oxford tomorrow,' said Felicity. 'I'm going to stay overnight with Gilla again and I'm having dinner with Josh.'

'With Josh, that bastard, what on earth for?'

'I've thought about it a lot since we spoke,' said

Felicity, 'and I think you're right, I think it must have been Josh who told Michael Ferguson about Dad and what I want to do is to ensure that he tells no one else, ever.'

'And how are you going to do that,' Mel asked, 'cut him through with the steak knife?'

'Very probably, but I thought if I was able to silence him once and for all on the subject then maybe ...,' she hesitated.

'Maybe you and I should keep it our secret,' Mel finished.

'Yes.'

'I am starting to grow up and calm down, Mum. I'm sorry my reaction was so over the top. I'm a lawyer, I should understand the frailties of the average human being. I do appreciate that none of us are perfect and there is no reason why I should have presumed that Dad was the exception.'

'And he paid a terrible price for what he did,' Felicity said, 'the ultimate price, too high a price for the nature of the crime.'

'I'd like it if we kept it to ourselves,' said Mel, 'and I think Dad would have liked that, too.'

Felicity left for Oxford at half past five the following morning, cursing the way the days were drawing in. It was pitch dark as she drove up the hill out of St Ives. It was strange, she thought, as she joined the Hayle bypass, driving to Oxford no longer felt like going home. When she left St Ives she felt as if she was tearing up her roots, stretching the umbilical cord – it was an extraordinary thing. She had lived in Oxford all her married life and in St Ives for only eighteen months. What did it mean, had she never really settled in Oxford? No, surely not, she had been happy there, raised her children there, had plenty of friends. She supposed it was because St Ives felt like her spiritual home – it was the atmosphere she adored – the different strands that came together to create such a cosmopolitan society – the artists, the writers, the fishermen, the wide variety of little businesses all trying to survive, the incomers, the indigenous Cornish who were so generous with their town. Then there were the contrast in the seasons – the madness of the summer months, the town heaving with holidaymakers; restaurants, pubs, shops working around the clock to support the all too short season, the proprietors becoming more and more hollow-eyed as the weeks went by; and then the winter months when St Ives shrank back to being a village again, when you couldn't walk down Fore Street without stopping every few minutes for a chat with someone you knew. She just loved it.

Felicity made good time to the M5/M4 junction, it was only just after nine, at this rate she would be in Oxford just after ten and could do some shopping. She might ring Gilla and see if she was free for lunch.

Then everything changed – The A46, Bath Junction 18 was ahead and suddenly Felicity realised she had to take it. The thought came to her out of a clear blue sky. On the way up, she had thought not at all about the Hopes. Having listened to John Humphries tear people apart on the Today Programme for as long as she could stand it, she had tuned to Radio 3 and thought a lot about Mel and her future and what on earth she was going to say to Josh Buchanan to ensure his silence. Yet here she was turning off towards Bath with a sudden, very strong feeling that she needed to go and see George and the Greshams. She stopped at the first available lay-by and checked her watch. Yes, Josh would be at work. She telephoned him, and after the usual wrangle with his impossible receptionist, was put through.

'Can you give me the Gresham's address?' she asked without preamble.

'Why?' Josh asked.

'Because I'm going to see them.'

'I thought you were coming to see me.'

'I am but that's not until later. Please Josh, I'm in a hurry.' The last thing she wanted to do was become involved in a lengthy chat – she was too cross with him. He gave her the address.

'I'll see you later then,' he said sounding puzzled.

'Absolutely,' said Felicity and rang off.

Half an hour later Felicity turned through the gates of Juniper Farmhouse and was rewarded by the sight of George playing on the lawn in front of the house with two chocolate coloured Labradors. She parked the car and got out. He looked up squinting in the sunlight.

'Hello Fizzy,' he said. 'I was hoping I'd see you again.'

'Well that's a very nice greeting, thank you,' said Felicity. 'I've been hoping I'd see you again, too. Who are these splendid people?'

'Whisky and Soda,' said George. 'They're brothers. Whisky is the soppy one and Soda is the one who just loves water.' He rolled Whisky onto his back to demonstrate the soppiness. 'Dad died,' he said, in the alarming way children have of being so completely straightforward.

'I heard, I'm terribly sorry George, I can see you're being very brave about it.'

George looked up biting his bottom lip. 'I get to live with Granny and Gramps.'

'That's really good isn't it?'

George nodded. 'I'm going to be a farmer when I grow up.'

'And a very good farmer you'll be, I'm sure,' said Felicity.

There was a crunch on the gravel and they looked up to see Clara walking towards them. 'Mrs Paradise,' she said, 'how nice to see you.' She held out her hand but while her greeting appeared genuine, a cloud seemed to cross her face. That's why I'm here, Felicity thought, because of that cloud.

'George has been asking about you,' Clara said.

'He's just told me, I feel very flattered. He's just been introducing me to Whisky and Soda, they're wonderful. I'd like a dog one day but at the moment my life is ruled by an aged, extremely bad-tempered cat called Orlando.'

George looked up and smiled with interest. 'Is he a marmalade cat?'

'Of course,' said Felicity, 'you must come and see him one day.'

Clara and Felicity went inside leaving George playing with the dogs. 'Would you like some coffee?' Clara asked.

'Yes, please,' said Felicity.

'Come along to the kitchen then.'

'How is George doing?' Felicity asked.

'You've heard about Philip, I suppose?' Felicity nodded. 'Did George say anything to you about his father?'

'Yes, he did,' said Felicity. 'but not much. He just told me that his father was dead and I said I was sorry and he said that it meant he could live with you and your husband. It was quite a matter-of-fact conversation.'

'There have been a few tears but he seems to be taking it in his stride. To lose both his parents, however unsatisfactory they may have been, is a terrible burden for a little boy to cope with in such a short space of time. I just wonder what long-term damage it will do.'

'With you and your husband to look after him and cherish him, I'm sure he will be fine,' said Felicity, meaning it.

Clara stared at her, drinking in the reassurance. 'I hope you're right.'

'I'm a school teacher,' said Felicity to lighten the mood, 'of course I'm right.' Both women laughed.

'I'll just take George out a juice and a biscuit,' said Clara, 'and then we can settle down in the morning room. He's going up to the farm in a moment to help move the cows from one field to another, he loves it up there.'

On Clara's return, the two women went through to the morning room and sat down by the window. 'It's very nice to see you Mrs Paradise, did you come for any reason in particular?'

'I'm not sure, quite,' said Felicity.

Clara frowned and Felicity could feel her withdrawing. 'That's a rather odd thing to say, isn't it?'

'Yes,' said Felicity. She took a sip of coffee to steady herself to try and put into words what she was thinking. 'Over the last year or so I've worked quite closely with Inspector Penrose,' she said, 'he's in charge of your daughter's murder case.'

'I know who Inspector Penrose is, Mrs Paradise.' Clara's voice was heavy with sarcasm.

'Yes, of course, I'm sorry I'm not thinking straight. Inspector Penrose also found the person who was responsible for killing my husband. It was a deliberate hit and run.'

'I'm so sorry,' said Clara, sounding genuine, 'I really am, but I don't see where this is leading.'

'Neither do I, quite. It's just that Inspector Penrose is stuck. There is no obvious motive for the murder of your daughter and no likely murderer.'

'It's his job to find out who killed her,' Clara said, 'I don't see why you're involved.'

'Neither do I, but, tell me, Mrs Gresham, do you have a theory?' Felicity asked.

'Not a theory exactly, but I suppose I think it was just a passing stranger, somebody she upset or who upset her – a terrible accident.'

'The police think she died in Malpas, which is hardly Moss Side,' Felicity said. 'I think you could probably walk through Malpas in the middle of the night, dripping in diamonds and minks with a hundred thousand pounds in your pocket and be quite safe, which is one of the reasons Inspector Penrose believes it was a crime of passion.' Clara said nothing, but Felicity could not give up now. 'I suppose what I am saying is that I don't understand why you appear so disinterested in who murdered your daughter. I have a daughter, younger than Lizzie, but grown up. If she was murdered, I wouldn't rest until I found out who had done it and seen him bought to justice. It's like you are trying to protect somebody and I suppose I just came here today to see if I could help.'

'And how do you think you can do that, Mrs Paradise?' Clara's voice had an icy edge to it.

'I think you should tell me who killed your daughter and between us we should work out what to do about it.' There was no point in beating about the bush, Felicity realised. It was time for shock tactics.

There was a tense pause, then, 'If I knew that, Mrs Paradise, I would have told the police, naturally.'

Felicity ignored her. 'Would it be a good starting point if I told you that I know Philip Hope wasn't George's father?'

Clara gasped. 'How on earth could you know a thing like that? No one knows, no one at all except me, and Lizzie of course. How could you know? Were you friends with Lizzie, did she tell you?'

'No,' said Felicity. 'I only met her that once, the time I failed you all.'

'Is this why you're here, continuing to meddle in our family affairs to try and put the record straight?'

'Maybe,' Felicity admitted, 'but that doesn't mean I don't genuinely want to help. I know you're keeping something to yourself, and the strain of it, is just awful for you, I can see it. Tell me, does any of this have anything to do with Chris Bailey?'

'Chris Bailey?' Clara made an attempt to look baffled but Felicity could sense her rising panic. She pressed home her advantage.

'You know Chris Bailey. He owns the chandlery in Fore Street. I understand from him he's known your family for years and he seems to have a particular interest in George. Why's that, Mrs Gresham?'

Clara was poised, on a knife edge, between telling her everything or throwing her out of the house. Felicity saw from her expression the moment the decision was made, and thanked God for it.

'Lizzie came down on holiday with us during the Summer of '94. She brought Megan but Philip was working, of course. She was drinking a lot, going out at night, staying out 'til all hours. We were worried sick but of course we were there to look after Megan. Her mother's behaviour upset Megan, though – it was a very difficult situation, but developing into a far more difficult one than we could ever have imagined.' Felicity dare not say anything for fear of interrupting the flow – she just nodded in a way she hoped was encouraging. 'Unknown to us, Lizzie was having an affair with a local man, and unknown to us during that holiday she fell pregnant with George.'

'Who was the father.' Felicity dared say.

'You're right, of course, it was Chris Bailey.'

It had been no more than a hunch, a lucky guess that somehow Chris was involved, that his interest in the family was inappropriately intense. Felicity concentrated hard on not looking surprised.

'I think Chris killed Lizzie,' Clara said after a moment. 'I think she agreed to meet him in Truro. I expect the idea was that he picked her up from the train, they would talk and then he would deliver her to St Ives where she was going to meet up with my husband and George. I think Chris and Lizzie must have argued and I think he killed her. I loved my daughter, Mrs Paradise, but the effect of the drink over the years meant I came not to like her very much. She could be very manipulative and cruel, very self-absorbed. She wouldn't have cared at all about Chris's feelings. I think she would have just seen him as a means of getting George. I imagine realising he was being used in such a way would have devastated him. I do believe it's possible she just drove him too far.'

'Then why, oh why, haven't you told the police?' Felicity asked.

'Because if DNA proves that Chris is George's father, then there will be somebody else trying to disrupt George's life and perhaps take him away from us.'

'Not if Chris murdered your daughter.'

'But I don't know he did, I just believe he could have done. Before poor Philip died, I worried about what would happen if he found out that he wasn't George's father. I'm sure he had no idea he wasn't, but I didn't know how he would react to the knowledge – would he disown George or fight Chris for custody – he was such a cold, private man, I couldn't even guess at his reaction. All I did know was that it would cause yet more confusion, disruption and unhappiness in George's life. I thought the best thing was to leave things alone. Now George's parents are both dead, we've been told by our solicitor that we should be able to adopt him. However, by introducing Chris Bailey onto the scene, everything could go wrong again. If Chris is George's father and he didn't kill Lizzie then maybe George would have to go and live with him.'

'Let's start at the beginning again,' said Felicity, gently, 'tell me the whole story, every detail you can remember.'

Clara smiled at her, reached out and squeezed her hand. 'I think it's about time I stopped calling you Mrs Paradise.'

'George calls me Fizzy.'

'Fizzy!' she smiled slightly. 'Alright, I'll call you that. It would be such a tremendous relief to share this burden.'

'So I take it your husband doesn't know about Chris Bailey?'

'No,' said Clara, 'no one knows, that's why it has been such a nightmare, trying to decide alone what's best for George.'

14

She was on the motorway again heading not to Oxford, but back home to Cornwall. It had been a highly emotionally charged two hours but in the end Clara had agreed to tell Tom everything and while Felicity had sat alone in the morning room, the Greshams had decided that the police should be told of Chris Bailey's involvement with their family. They had one request.

'Could you tell Inspector Penrose everything?' Tom had asked. 'We've only had George home here for a couple of days. It would be terribly wrong to leave him at the moment. Also, it's his father's funeral tomorrow, we have to be together for that, it's a huge ordeal and we need to stay completely focused on supporting George.'

'If you're happy for me to tell him, of course I will. Maybe you should ring him and say I'm on my way and I have authority to speak on your behalf?'

'That's a good idea,' said Clara, 'we'll do that.'

'Even if Chris Bailey isn't responsible for your daughter's death,' Felicity said. 'I can't believe any court would ever take George away from you now. He's eight years old, he can't start again with a brand new relationship when he has you both to care for him.'

'I know what you say sounds logical but at three o'clock in the morning, nothing seems safe.'

'I know that feeling,' said Felicity.

Her mobile phone rang and she took the first exit to the Services and stopped the car. It was Keith Penrose.

'Hello, inspector.'

'I gather you are on your way down to see me with some breaking news, I assume you've solved the case.' He was being sarcastic, his voice was heavy with it.

'I think I might have done, yes.'

'Truly.'

'Truly.'

'Are you going to tell me about it?' The sarcasm had quite gone.

'Not on the telephone. I'm just about to join the A30. I should be with you within the next two hours.'

'Well, drive carefully,' said Penrose. 'If you're going to solve my murder for me I don't want you ending up in a heap of twisting metal before you can explain it all.'

'It's so nice to know you have my best interests at heart,' said Felicity.

'They met for the first time in his shop,' Felicity began. Penrose's office had reached a new level of awfulness. He'd had to move several great piles of paper for Felicity to even reach the chair. 'Lizzie and Chris Bailey, that is. He runs the chandlery in Fore Street, you must know him,' she burst out.

'I know the shop – but what's Chris Bailey got to do with anything?'

'He's George's father, Chris Bailey is George's father.'

'Dear God.'

'Lizzie and Megan were on holiday with the Greshams in St Ives. Megan had bought a little sailing boat and she wanted some string so she could sail it in the harbour. Mother and daughter went to the chandlery. Chris and Lizzie got talking, there was obviously immediate chemistry and Lizzie was able to go out at night because she had her parents to babysit. She met Chris every evening, they drank too much of course, ended up in bed and she became pregnant.'

'And Philip Hope never knew?'

'Apparently not,' said Felicity. 'She went home and managed to convince him that the child was his. Lizzie and her parents came down with Megan for one more holiday before the birth, I don't know whether Lizzie was trying to keep the relationship going with Chris – none of us will ever know now. At the time Clara herself had no idea about the nature of the relationship with Chris Bailey. She knew he was part of the group that Lizzie went out with at night, but that's all. While they were on holiday, Lizzie went into labour and was rushed to Treliske Hospital, the general message being put about was that the baby was early, although, in fact, George was born quite a respectable weight. Chris Bailey turned up shortly after the delivery demanding to see Lizzie and that was how Clara found out about the relationship. It's sad in a way. Mother, father and son only had a few hours together before Philip arrived to collect his family and take George home to raise as his own. I've been wondering driving down whether it was that sad and only meeting which could have turned Chris Bailey into a killer – spending that time playing families and then to have it so cruelly snatched away from him, for good – until that is, eight years later when Lizzie needed him for her custody battle.'

'You don't know he is a killer, do you?' Keith frowned.

'Not yet, no, but it fits, inspector.'

'If you say so – what happened next?'

'Two years later Megan died, the family split up, Lizzie lost George as well and, as far as Clara is aware, she had no further contact with Chris Bailey. We're only guessing here, but in recent months, as you know, Lizzie had cleaned up her act. She was no longer drinking and she wanted to make a bid to see more of George, see him or even regain custody of him. We think, or rather Clara thinks, that Lizzie was trying to enlist the help of Chris Bailey. If they could prove that George was in fact Chris's child, not Philip's, and Lizzie could demonstrate that she was now sober, there was a chance that they might obtain custody of the boy. I understand Lizzie was haunted by the fact that George was so unhappy and lonely with Philip.'

'So you think they met in Malpas?'

'Clara thinks – remember, inspector, this is Clara's story not mine – that Lizzie had arranged for Chris to pick her up off the train at Truro and for them to talk. I know no one saw them but as you have said, it was the busy commuter train, the Golden Hind.'

'But why not come onto St Ives, why did Lizzie get out at Truro?'

'Maybe she wanted to meet on neutral ground – her father and son were in St Ives, remember. Clara had contacted Lizzie when they had taken George away from home and told her where he was. Maybe that was the trigger – George was in St Ives, Chris was in St Ives, maybe that was what made her think out the plan to enlist Chris's help, but she never confided in her mother. Anyway, Clara believes Lizzie thought it was probably best to meet away from St Ives to talk the whole thing through first. She reckons Chris picked her up from Truro station, took her out to the Heron at Malpas and then they argued. Clara admitted that Lizzie could be cruel and unfeeling at times and I know from personal experience that Chris Bailey has a very short temper. He may have been goaded into losing control.'

'It certainly fits in with my crime of passion theory,' said Inspector Penrose.

'Chris was probably incredibly bitter – first Lizzie cut him out of their son's life to preserve her marriage and then when it suited her, she wanted to enlist his help. Then there is the issue of Megan's death – he may well have been very reluctant to help her get her hands on George, even if it meant he could see his son, after what happened to Megan.'

'And why have the Greshams not told us all this before?'

'Only Clara knew the whole story and she was afraid it would be another factor which could lose them George. She was terrified of the little boy having any more disruption in his life. It makes sense, inspector.'

Keith let out a sigh. 'It's eight o'clock now,' he said. 'I think it's best Jack and I pay Mr Bailey a visit first thing in the morning. You don't know where he lives, do you?'

'I've no idea,' said Felicity, 'but he opens his shop relatively early. You should get him there about half past eight I reckon.' Felicity frowned, 'Did you say it was eight o'clock.' Keith nodded. 'Oh blast!'

'What's wrong?' Keith asked.

'I was supposed to meet Josh Buchanan for dinner in Oxford and I've just stood him up.'

'Do you want to use my phone to ring him?' Keith asked.

'No thanks,' said Felicity with a grin, 'let him sit there and stew.'

At eight thirty the following morning, Inspector Keith Penrose and Sergeant Jack Curnow presented themselves at Bailey's Chandlers. Chris Bailey was behind the counter.

'We'd like to talk to you, sir , about the death of Lizzie Hope.'

'Who?' said Chris Bailey.

'I think that was your first mistake, sir,' said Inspector Penrose. 'You know who Lizzie Hope is, you know the Hope family, you told Mrs Paradise as much. We also know that George Hope is your son.'

'I don't know what you mean?' said Chris Bailey. As he spoke he raised his hands in a gesture of innocence –his hands appeared to be covered in white cotton gloves. Keith stared at them.

'Can I ask why you're wearing gloves, sir?'

'Yes,' said Chris, looking confused. 'It's the nickel, it gives me dermatitis, I have to wear these most of the time. I'm in the wrong trade, really.' He tried a smile but his nervousness was palpable. The final piece slipped into the jigsaw. A crime of passion at odds with the gloved hands used to strangle the victim. Inspector Penrose knew he had got his man.

14 June 2004 Oxford

The sun shone on the Gresham family and their special guests as they walked from the County Court down Cornmarket to the Randolph Hotel. The sun shone, and so it should, for moments before the judge had ordered the adoption of George Alexander Hope, now to be known by his mother's maiden name of George Gresham. The adoptive parents, also his grandparents, would find themselves in something of a conundrum the judge joked – Granny or Mummy, Dad or Granddad – the only person who seemed remotely interested in this was the judge. No one else cared who was called what – for George was safe at last.

In the private room at the Randolph, the adoption party was in full swing, when Tom Gresham rose to his feet.

'I have a number of people to thank,' said Tom, 'people who made today possible, but firstly I would like you to all remember our daughter, Lizzie, George's mother, who gave life to this very splendid young man we see before us today.' The room sobered immediately.

'To Lizzie,' everyone said, raising their glass.

'Secondly, I would like to thank the police for all their help in untangling our very complicated and often tragic family problems, and in particular Detective Inspector Keith Penrose for his very sympathetic and tactful handling of our case. Inspector Penrose.'

Everyone raised their glass, Keith looked bashful Felicity noticed with amusement.

'I would also like to thank Felicity Paradise who risked life and limb stumbling about on the cliffs in the dark and who found George when he had successfully eluded both the police and Culdrose Air/Sea Rescue. Felicity, this family owes you a very great deal.'

She heard the toast, she felt tears well into her eyes and as Tom began to speak again, she slipped from the room and dashed to the Ladies. 'This family owes you a very great deal.' She mulled the words over as she stared at her reflection in the mirror, trying ineffectually to stem the tears falling down her face. He had no idea how much the words meant to her, but then again, perhaps he did.

Keith Penrose found Felicity sitting alone in the

bar a few minutes later.

'There you are,' he said, 'I'm not going to ask you if you'd like a drink, I'm going to tell you you're to have one.' He ordered some wine and then came and sat beside her. 'A good day?' he ventured.

Felicity smiled at him, 'Yes, it is.'

'So why are you sitting here all alone, looking like you're on the verge of tears?'

'Too much emotion I suppose. It was odd being back in the Oxford County Court, the last time I was there was for Charlie's inquest.'

'Of course,' said Keith, 'I should have thought of that, I'm sorry.'

Felicity shook her head. 'It was such a happy occasion, it was good in a way, helped counteract the past.'

'So what else is wrong?' Keith asked.

'Nothing's wrong, quite the contrary, really. Tom Gresham is a nice man, he said just the right thing, didn't he?'

'Just the right thing,' Keith agreed.

'I've been wanting to speak to you ever since seeing you in court, inspector. How is Carly?'

'Not out of the wood yet, but much better. The treatment, harsh though it was, certainly seems to have got the cancer on the run. Carly is very positive about life at the moment, and so are Barbara and I as a result.'

'I'm pleased,' said Felicity.

'Carly is going to retrain as a physiotherapist. She's spent so much time in hospital she has become interested in helping people. Sport as a career is not really on for her at the moment, but physio is a natural extension.'

'It will be really good for her,' said Felicity, 'getting stuck into something new.'

'Yes, she is very enthusiastic about it, and how's your daughter?'

'Mel is fine. She has been taken on by a firm in Exeter; she has decided to go into family law. She is still seeing Martin regularly, but there's no talk yet of a firm commitment. She's loving her job though.'

'Do you know if they've told George about the identity of his father?'

Felicity nodded. 'Yes, they knew he would find out one day so they thought it was better to tell him straight away. He's had counselling and while obviously it's terrible to have to cope with the knowledge that your birth father murdered your mother, I think it helped that Chris confessed so quickly and was so obviously filled with remorse. It really was your 'crime of passion' wasn't it – his temper reacted like a tinderbox to so much emotion. He did a terrible thing but at least the Greshams were able to tell George that his father isn't a monster. George is a resilient little chap.'

'I suppose the scars will come up to the surface during the teenage years,' Keith said, 'that's usually

282

when we have to face all the mistakes we've made in raising them.'

'Certainly that's when we get told what we've done wrong,' said Felicity, smiling. 'The degree of intensive care necessary to raise these children of ours and keep them safe and happy – it's a nightmare.'

'Would you have it any other way?' asked Keith.

'No, of course not,' said Felicity.

'Then let us raise our glasses,' said Keith, 'in a private toast to George Gresham, may he have a long and happy life.' Keith took a sip of his wine and without saying a word or even glancing in Felicity's direction, he felt in his breast pocket and handed her his handkerchief.